TEPOZTECO'S BELLY

By José Agustín

Translated by Nicolás Kanellos

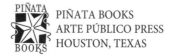

PIÑATA BOOKS
ARTE PÚBLICO PRESS
HOUSTON, TEXAS

Arte Público Press thanks Alaíde Ventura Medina and Travis A. Bryson for their careful editing.

Piñata Books are full of surprises!

Piñata Books

An imprint of
Arte Público Press
University of Houston
4902 Gulf Fwy, Bldg 19, Rm 100
Houston, Texas 77204-2004

Cover design by Ryan Hoston
Cover art and halftones by José Agustín Ramírez

Printed in the United States of America

October 2023–November 2023
Versa Press, Inc., East Peoria, IL
5 4 3 2 1

For Tino who recently emerged from these territories, and for Carlitos Frontera Lloreda

Contents

I

"Look at this, they're packed like sardines," Yanira exclaimed, pouting. "I told you we should have bought the tickets yesterday!"

"Right, what a downer," chubby Thor said, snorting.

The seven kids had just arrived at the southern bus terminal, which was crowded with travelers.

"It's because of the holiday," Erika explained matter-of-factly. "These days are beautiful and everyone wants to get out of the city."

"Jeez," Alaín squealed, "any tickets left?"

All seven of them looked around as they sped up, carrying their luggage through the crowd of people standing in long lines at each ticket counter. Homero was bringing up the rear, listening to his Walkman. They reached the other side of the terminal, where they sold tickets for the Cristóbal Colón bus line.

"Ach!" Yanira exclaimed, "look at that line!"

"Yep, it's unending!" Erika said. "You all need to get in line while I go ask what times the buses are leaving. Selene, you get in line," she instructed the youngest of the group, an eight-year-old.

"Me, by myself?" Selene asked, looking at the mass of people.

"I'll stay with her," Thor volunteered. "I'll take care of her. I'll take care of you, kiddo."

Selene nodded in agreement and pulled out a stick of gum. "You want a some?" she asked Thor.

"Of course."

"I'll go ask what time the buses are leaving," Alaín said.

"No, I'll go," Erika butted in.

"Well, let's the both of us go," Alaín settled it.

They both made their way through the crowd lining up until they reached the ticket counter.

"What time do . . . ?"

". . . the buses leave for Tepoztlán?" Erika finished Alaín's sentence.

"At twelve-thirty," a clerk's rough voice answered without looking at them.

"*At twelve-thirty?*" Erika and Alaín repeated, aghast.

"Or even later, if you don't get in line right away," the clerk threatened. "Get in line, kids, or the schedule may be canceled, and you won't be able to go nowhere."

"But, it's not even eight a.m. yet. It's more than three hours until twelve-thirty," Erika complained.

"*Four hours*," Alaín corrected her.

"Get in line, now, rascals."

Erika and Alaín slowly returned to the line where the others were waiting.

"Guess what?" Alaín started to say.

"They only have tickets for the twelve-thirty departure," Erika finished his thought.

"Not until twelve-thirty?" Thor repeated, skeptical. "You've got to be joking."

"Nope."

"What'll we do?" interjected Erika. "If we wait *here* for four hours, we'll get to Tepoz who knows when."

"At two in the afternoon," Alaín specified.

"*Four hours?*" Thor repeated.

"What do we do?" Erika repeated, deflated.

"Let's call my dad," Thor suggested. "He said to call him if we encountered any problems."

"Oh, the little baby," Erika said, "he can't do anything without his daddy."

"Well, what do you suggest we do?"

"And what about Homer?"

"He's in back of the line wearing his earphones."

"You want a piece of bubble gum, Erika?" asked Selene, who had only moved up five centimeters in the long line.

"Sure," Erika accepted it.

"Listen up, everybody. Wait!" shouted Yanira, who emerged from the crowd.

"Where have you been?" Alaín asked her.

"You can get lost. . . ." Erika added.

"She always disappears," Thor said.

"It's the Lone Yanira," Homero added.

"Oh, be quiet, all of you. Listen to me."

"Okay, but don't shout."

"Look, while all of you were here like sticks in the mud, I went over and found out what we can do."

They all took a few moments to look at her, and Yanira proudly stood her ground with all eyes on her.

"Well, what?" asked Erika, impatiently.

"What do I get if I tell you?"

"Man, you're really milking it. . . ."

"Well, we're going to take a *combi*."

"A *combi*? What *combi*? Are you crazy?" Alaín said.

"They leave from just outside, down the stairs by the entrance to the Metro. They go to Tepoztlán, Oaxtepec and Cuautla. They depart as soon as they fill up. Each ticket costs twenty pesos. Whad'ya say?" Yanira asked with a beaming smile.

They were all speechless.

"Oh, and they're not exactly *combis*. . . . They're minibuses, like the ones you see everywhere these days."

"Are you sure about this?" Erika asked.

"Yep."

"How do you know all this?" Alaín asked.

"Because some men in line were talking. I heard them and so I asked, and they explained it all to me. And they've already gone to board the minibus. Let's go, okay?"

"Let's go," Thor declared.

"Wait a minute," Alaín interrupted. "What if it's bad info? Someone should stay in line here so we don't lose our place."

"What for?" Yanira protested. "There's still seats in the minibuses, and they're leaving now."

"Let's have Selene, Homero, Indra, Thor and Yanira stay in line," ordered Erika without paying any attention to Yanira. "I'll go check it out."

"No, I'll go," said Alaín.

"Let's go together," countered Erika.

"I want to go . . ." Selene begged, ". . . I'm tired of standing here."

"No, Selene, you're too small, you stay here," ordered Erika.

"No way, I want to go."

"Oh, let her come," Alaín decided. "I'll take care of her."

Erika huffed but accepted it. Alaín took the little girl by the hand, and the three of them made their way through the crowd and into the street.

"People are still arriving, you see that?" Alaín observed.

"Why are there so many people?" Selene asked.

"Because of the holiday," Alaín explained.

"But why?"

"Oh, Selene, didn't they teach you anything in school?" Erika asked impatiently.

They were already outside where bunches of cars and buses were passing slowly in front of the terminal. They headed for the minibuses lined up around the Taxqueña Metro station.

"Because September fifteenth and the sixteenth are when Mexican independence is celebrated, and this year they fall on Thursday and Friday," Alaín explained. "And they're followed by Saturday and Sunday, so that's four days in a row when there's no school and everyone can have plenty of time to party."

"Just like us, dummy!" Erika said.

They got to where a group of minibuses were parked, along with numerous other passenger vehicles heading to different parts of Mexico City. People were streaming in and out of the Metro station. Indeed that the minibuses were leaving as soon as they filled up, and that they were headed for Cuautla and Oaxtepec. They weren't going into Tepoztlán proper, but would let passengers off at the bus stop just outside of town.

"And from there, we can get a taxi or a *combi* into town," Erika exclaimed. "Let's do it. We're seven," she said as she took out some bills and counted them carefully as she handed them to the minibus driver. "Alaín, hotfoot it over to get the others. Your stay with me, Selene."

Alaín hesitated for a second. He hated taking orders, especially those coming from Erika, but he took off running through the crowds, the cars and minibuses that were spewing exhaust into the morning air. Erika and Selene boarded the minibus, which already had some passengers: a married couple that looked like they were peasants, a man who looked like a poor teacher—Erika imagined and various other types of people, more accurately old people. One of the senior citizens talked and talked and the other just listened. Erika and Selene sat down on two seats and informed the people boarding that those other two were "occupied."

"Yes, those girls paid for seven tickets," the driver confirmed as he continued to sell tickets at the bus' door.

Erika gave the young driver a defiant look. She couldn't stand being called a girl, simply because she no longer considered herself one at thirteen years of age and was already in high school. She was a teenager, as her mother said, and if she wore makeup and her sister Myriam's high heels, she could get in anywhere.

The minibus had filled up, except for the two benches reserved by Erika and Selene, and neither Alaín nor Thor nor Indra nor Homero nor Yanira had arrived. Some of the passengers were already complaining, "Let's hit the road" and "It's getting late" and "Yes, let's go, let's go already, driver."

"No! Wait!" Erika clamored in anguish.

"I'll go look for them, Erika," Selene volunteered.

"You? You've gotta be kiddin'. You'll get lost. No, I better go."

"Let's go-o-o-o!" passengers were shouting.

"You? And what if you don't get back?" Selene worried.

"What do you mean *if I don't get back*? Of course, I'll get back. Darn! I hate them! What could be taking them so long?"

"Let's get going!" the passengers were insisting.

The driver, already sitting behind the steering wheel, didn't pay them any attention and just passively observed the intense movement of the masses of people and the vehicles around the Metro station and the bus terminal.

"Selene, I'm going to go look for them. You wait here, stay calm, and nothing will happen. These adults will watch out for you, and I'll go like a flash to see what's going on . . ."

Erika paused because at that moment there seemed to be a ruckus outside, and then Alaín boarded the bus.

"We're here," he announced.

"What a mess," exclaimed Homero.

"It was all because of Indra," Thor pointed a finger.

"It wasn't my fault!"

"Shhhhhhh!"

"I told you we shouldn't have stayed in line. It was dumb. After all, we were going in the *combi*."

"Be quiet already!"

"Pain-in-the-butt kids!"

"Let's go, already!"

"Sit down, now, and don't make so much noise," the driver ordered.

"Uhhhh," some murmured, while others laughed.

The driver ignored them, put the minibus in gear and took off as best he could go into the traffic moving at snail's pace in front of the southern bus terminal.

More and more people were still pouring into the area.

"God!" Indra exclaimed, "I thought we'd never get out of there."

"Well, now you see, we're okay," Alaín said.

"I told you that we should have all come together to the *combi*," Yanira insisted. "There was no reason for us to stay back there in line."

"It's not a *combi*, it's a minibus," Alaín corrected her.

"Hey, Homero, lend me your Walkman," Thor asked.

"He doesn't even hear you," Indra reminded him. "Anyway, you have your own."

"Yes, but not on me."

"Now, can you explain why it took you all so long to get here?" Erika asked.

". . . And anyway, your Walkman is much cooler."

"It was because dumb-head Indra went to make a phone call," Yanira explained. "I told her not to go, but she always does whatever she wants."

"It was an important call . . ." murmured Indra with an embarrassed smile.

"And why the heck could you not hurry up?" challenged Thor.

"Language!" someone in back said.

"Shhh, don't curse," Yanira said. "Who did you call, Indra?"

"Rubén . . . I promised I'd call him whenever I could."

"What! I thought it was supposed to be an *important* call!"

"Well, it was important. . . ."

"You get it, Homero?"

"What?" Homero said as he took off the headphones.

"You know why Indra took so long? Because she was talking to her boyfriend," said Thor.

"She's so stupid," Homero said and put the headphones back on.

"But why did you take so long, Indra?" Selene asked. "We waited forever for you, and these people here wanted to kill us."

"Be QUIET already," someone in back shouted.

"They sound like a bunch of parakeets!"

"It was because all the telephones in the bus terminal were out of order or had long lines waiting to use them. . . ."

"So, what did you do?"

"I went down to use the telephone at the Metro station."

"So that's why we couldn't find you. . . ." Thor exclaimed.

"ENOUGH!" all the other passengers shouted.

"SHUT UP!"

"Shhhh!"

"Don't pay attention to them," Erika told Yanira. "They have also been blabbing, blah, blah, blah."

"I know," Yanira answered. "Did you see that old man? He just keeps blabbing and blabbing, all like angry and red in the face."

"I bet they're talking politics."

"Oh yeah, bo-o-o-oring. . . . Hey, I like your pants. Are they from the States?"

"Yes, Yani, and guess what. Our creepy school principal chewed me out for wearing them to class, 'cause he said they were too tight. He was even going to call my mom. And she was the one who bought them for me in Houston!"

They both broke into laughter.

"He's an idiot," Yanira summed it up.

"What are you two talking about?" Indra broke in.

"The principal."

"My God, what's up with you two! Talk about something positive."

"It's you, Indra, that needs God's pardon. These old people were about to lynch us because you all were holding us up."

"Oh, Erika, you sound like my mother."

"You want some gum, Indra?" Selene offered.

"Sure, hand it over."

They had already left the city, but there was still a lot of traffic. There was an interminable line of cars, *combis*, minibuses and buses at the highway toll booth. Behind them could be seen the heavy cloud of pollution hanging over the city. It was really noticeable, because the sky in front of them was clear blue.

"Man, what a mob," Thor commented.

The girls broke out in laughter to the immediate response of "Shhh," "Cackling hens," "Shut up already," which would be echoed during the whole trip.

"I wish we were already in Tepoz," Alaín said. "My dad is gonna freak out when he sees I've arrived with this bunch."

"Whoa! You mean you didn't warn him?"

"Well, all I said was that I might bring some friends . . ." Alaín confessed with a shy smile, "but not how many. Anyway, he said, 'Bring whomever you wish.'"

"Oh, okay, then."

"I was only going to invite you and Homero, but then Erika heard us discussing it in the school yard . . . remember?"

"Yes, I do, and she immediately signed up."

"And I said, okay, sure, come along, right? And then Homero liked the idea, but what I really think is that he likes her, smarty pants that she is."

"Wow! She's horrible and now that she wears braces . . ."

"And then Erika said her parents wouldn't let her go to Tepoztlán with just *guys*, and so I told her to bring along a girlfriend . . . but, man, I never thought she'd invite Yanira and Indra and even that short-stuff Selene."

"I like that little girl. But, won't your dad get angry?"

"Maybe . . . it depends what mood he's in. If he's good, perfect, but if not, it doesn't matter because he'll be locked away in his study, and even my mother won't see him."

"How about your mother?"

"My mother left yesterday. She didn't want us to come home by ourselves, 'cause she said we were too young to travel alone, you know, crazy stuff like that. But I told her it was no big deal, that it's so easy to take the bus to Tepoz. In the end, she wasn't happy, but she had to go see a lady about a cleansing."

"A what?"

"A witch. . . . Haven't you ever seen one?"

"A witch? Are you crazy, man? You've seen witches?"

"In Tepoz there's a bunch of them. Well . . . but they're not like cartoons, you know, with broomstick and everything. They're more like indigenous old ladies who rub you all over with tree branches and eggs while they pray and pray."

"For real?"

"Yep. Take my word for it. My mom really gets into that stuff. When I was a kid, she took me a few times so that they'd cleanse me."

"What does it feel like?"

"What are you guys talking about?" Homero asked after taking off the headphones.

"Whoa! Even this guy put the Walkman aside to hear this," commented Thor, jealously spying the apparatus Homero had clipped to his pants' belt.

"So, what were you talking about?"

"Witches."

"Witches?"

"Yeah, sure, who do you think you're kiddin'?" Homero said as he put the headphones back on.

Thor took them from Homero for a moment. "You'll lend them to me a little later, okay?"

Homero nodded in agreement.

"My mom loves astrology and has her cards read," Thor said.

"Yeah, my mom, too, but in addition she really gets carried away with the witches in Tepoztlán. Every so often, they do some things for her, and they cleanse her and give her herbs and talismans and a bunch of other stuff. Then she goes to the Tepozteco temple, saying she has to pay tribute to Tepozteco at least once a year. The hill there is really cool, like something out of *Indiana Jones*. You've been up to Tepozteco Hill, right?"

"Of course, dude. With you."

"Soon we'll be going up again, right?"

"You bet. But before that, we need to get some Nintendo in. I've got some cool games on loan."

"Hey, man, Thor, you spend all your time on those games, and now even when you're going out to the countryside you want to be shut in playing games?! You should have your head examined, Héctor."

"My name is Thor."

"Yeah, if you say so."

"Oh, all right, first we go up to Tepozteco and then I'll show you *The Incredible Labyrinths of Borges*, it's super cool. And Homero also brought some games, but they're the same old ones."

"Cool."

"My mom didn't want to let me come, 'cause my grades have been the pits. And she doesn't like me going anywhere by myself, but even less with a bunch of guys, and even less with girls. She really talked bad about your mom and dad because they leave us alone."

"What's wrong with that? I've been taking the bus since I was eleven or younger. And my sister, when we lived in Tepoz and she was ten, she took the bus to go everywhere, by herself without asking anyone's permission . . . she'd go to Cuautla, Yautepec, Cuernavaca . . . once even to Taxco. Can you believe it?"

"Yes, your sister is really somethin'. And your mom is also pretty crazy, don't you think?"

"What's wrong with you?! Don't dis my mom."

"And your dad . . ."

"What about my dad?"

"I mean, what's up with him?"

"He's usually a good guy, you know him. Now he's working on a project that he's spent a whole week on in the Tepoztlán house. My mom just got to see him a while yesterday, and my sister is off to Guadalajara with her little girlfriends."

"Yeah, that's what you said."

The girls kept up the laughter despite the continuing protests from the other passengers. Alaín and Thor looked back at them, and Homero took off the headphones. The girls were singing popular songs, adding off-color interpretations by adding "in the front" and "from behind."

"I really want you—" Erika sang.

"—in the front . . ."

"I can't get rid of you—"

"—from behind . . ."

"Because it's just the same . . ."

"—in the front . . ."

"I need you—."

"—from behind . . ."

"I want to feel your love—"

"—in the front . . ."

"And feel your warmth—."

"—from behind . . ."

"With this need for you—"

"—in the front . . ."

"When you're close to me—"

"—from behind . . ."

"That's overdone already, don't you think?" Yanira protested. "Why don't you sing something more soothing?"

"The National Anthem!" Homero proposed, laughing.

"They're all the same," declared Indra.

"Well, for creating lyrics . . . ," Thor said.

"For sweet little songs," Homero commented as he put his headphones back on.

Now, the guys were laughing out loud, followed by renewed shouts of "Shut up," "Jerks," etc.

"Ooooh!" yelled the seven kids.

"That's enough! If you don't pipe down, we're gonna take you to the police station," a furious passenger threatened.

"Ooooh!" everyone shouted again and laughed.

"Shut up now!" a passenger insisted, stood up and started staggering forward down the minibus' aisle. "You all shut up or I'll take my belt to you!" he roared.

"Sit down or you gonna fall, mister," Homero told him.

"Please, mister, sit down," the driver ordered.

"Ooooh!" the kids shouted, when the upset passenger hobbled back to his seat, grumbling, but then the kids piped down.

"How much longer, Erika?" Selene asked.

"Not much, we've already passed the town of Tres Marías," Alaín responded.

"Here, an apple."

"Oh right, who has the sandwiches?" Indra asked.

"I've got them," Erika announced.

"Oh, brother, you always get your hands on everything," Indra complained.

"Well, it's because you finish everything. . . ."

"That's not true."

"Weren't there some hard-boiled eggs?"

"Watch out! Here comes the famous pear curve, Thor warned. And once they were driving through the dangerous curve, he took the opportunity to lean on Indra, who was sitting next to him. "My favorite curve!" he shouted.

"Get off me, fool! You weigh a lot!"

"And he smells even worse," Yanira added with a giggle.

"SHUT UP ALREADY!"

Coming out of the curve, the minibus driver took advantage of the downhill slope and accelerated to pass a few timid cars. Soon they saw the signs indicating the turnoff for Tepoztlán, Oaxtepec, Cuautla. The minibus didn't slow down on the well-traveled highway. At that early morning hour, the pine forest shined in the clear air and brilliant sun rising to its zenith. The kids did not even notice when the minibus pulled up to the Tepoztlán bus stop.

The other passengers could breathe again and voiced their sentiments: "About time!" "Now we can rest a bit." "Darn kids." "I couldn't put up with them a second longer." The only exception, Erika observed, was the passenger who was arguing about politics and had not stop talking since leaving the terminal in Mexico City.

"Now he's even angrier," she thought as she jumped down from the minibus. She also noticed that the driver was smiling warmly. *He was a really nice guy*, she said to herself.

The kids arrived at Alaín's house without much effort. From the bus stop they took a taxi driven by a dark-skinned boy who, some twenty years earlier, would have ridden a horse. They quickly drove through a series of curves and down the main street, which had as its backdrop the Tepozteco mountain range. On arriving, Alaín always enjoyed seeing the immense green wall that sparked his imagination and filled him with a sense of mystery. However, at this moment he was anxious to show his friends the town, the mountains, the people . . . all within five minutes.

"Look, there's the town square," Alaín pointed out.

"Ugh! It's ugly," said Yanira.

"And that's city hall. Down below is the marketplace. It's really hopping on weekends, you'll see."

"I've never been here," Indra said thoughtfully.

"I have," Erika said.

"The town's pretty small, huh?" Thor commented.

"Not so . . . well, it's a town, you know?"

"What is beautiful are the hills," Indra continued.

They left the main street and entered the Santo Domingo neighborhood via Jardineras Street, whose pavement was always horribly disrupted with pot holes full of water and large stones that had rolled down from the hills. But the little street was pretty, with wild plants sprouting out of every crack in the adobe and stone walls and cobblestone street.

"There goes Maciel," Alaín exclaimed, pointing to a solidly built, tall man who was in animated conversation with a woman who had a white streak in the middle of her hair and was wearing a long skirt.

"Who?" Yanira asked.

"He's a painter who lives in Tepoztlán," Alaín informed them. "He paints gigantic pictures of black women reclining in hammocks."

"I've never met a painter," Yanira said.

"I have," Erika affirmed.

"And the woman?"

"That's Beatriz . . . Marién and Sergio's mother. She makes beautiful dresses."

The girls, with the exception of Erika who was familiar with Tepoztlán, were captivated by the view of the town and the mountain. They also liked Alaín's house, which was a little odd, looking like an old Swiss chalet constructed on uneven terrain. Some of its rooms were small, dark and triangular, while others were gigantic, with high ceilings and bathed in light. The backyard was similarly arranged on different levels, was covered in vegetation and had a small pool. From there, the view of Tepozteco was very impressive.

Alaín's father was in good humor and happily welcomed the kids. "Why didn't you bring your teachers along?" he joked.

His mother, too, was happy to receive the visitors, especially since there were four girls in the group. "I'm used to living with just males in this house and I'm over it," she explained. "My name is Coral, which is what I want you to call me. No formalities."

The girls liked that very much but didn't give it a second thought because they were fawning over an attractive, older boy who was about to leave.

He greeted everyone and then said goodbye. "I'll talk to you later, Alaín," he said as he stepped out.

"Who was that?" Erika immediately asked, which caused Homero and Thor to flee as well.

"He's cute," Yanira said.

"That's Gonzalo. He lives around the corner and comes home on weekends, like I do. He lives just behind Perisur in Mexico City. We're friends, even though he's a lot older than me. We've known each other since I was tiny."

"How old is he?" asked Yanira, who seemed fascinated.

"Seventeen or eighteen, I'm not sure. He'll soon graduate from high school."

"Which school?"

"He's so handsome!" Yanira now pronounced.

"Yeah, but forget about it, he's got five years on you and won't give you a second look," Erika countered.

"Well, I can see you girls are not bored," Coral said as she brought in a tray with glasses of papaya juice. "Follow me," she said to the girls. "I'll show you where you're going to sleep. . . . And you boys are going to bed down in Alaín's room."

The girls followed Alaín's mother as they sipped their papaya juice.

"Where are the guys?" Alaín wondered as he came back to the living room. "Oh, yeah," he realized as he headed for his bedroom and found Homero and Thor already playing his video games, whose graphics were devilishly good.

"Yep, I thought I'd find you here."

"You're up next against me," Thor said without taking his eyes off the screen.

"I'm just a-bout to vap-o-rize this . . ." he chortled.

"Not so fast . . ." retorted Homero, "this poor chub is about to . . ."

Alaín realized they were not addressing him; they were so engaged in the *Los Contras* game that they weren't paying attention to him. Laughing to himself, he made his way between the two cots for the guests and flopped down on his bed. He enjoyed observing his friends from behind as they faced the screen, until they were called to wash their hands before dinner.

"Wait," Alaín said, "I'm gonna call Pancho. He's from here and knows the mountain better than anyone. They call him 'The Master of the Mountain,'" he proudly announced. "I'm not kidding," he emphasized to surprised stares.

"Let's all go by ourselves," Erika said. "Why do we need guides? You're familiar enough with the mountain, right?"

"Well, yes, but not like Pancho."

"Anyway, it's really easy," insisted Erika, "I've done it before, and the trail is easy to follow . . . and up higher, there's a metal ladder you need to climb."

"And who is Pancho, anyway?" Yanira asked.

"Must be the laundry woman's son, or something like that," Erika said.

"Look, Erika, if you liked my friend Gonzalo," Alaín insinuated with a glint in his eye, "when you see Pancho, your mouth will be watering. Both of them are really good friends, and when they go out on weekends, well, you wouldn't believe all the girls . . ."

"Really?"

"You got that right," Thor interjected. "I know him, and he's *cute*," he said, imitating Yanira.

There was no getting around Alaín's reasoning—Alaín and Thor were mimicking Erika—as they walked down a narrow street to a bridge over a risen stream rushing by very tall trees. They crossed the bridge to a stone wall enclosing horses and cows in front of a small adobe house shaded by trees on both sides.

"Does he live here?" Yanira asked.

"Pancho! Pancho-o-o-o!" Alaín called out.

"He's the washer woman's son," said Erika.

"No, he's the son of the woman who does the cleansings," Alaín, said, smiling.

"Oh darn," Yanira blurted out.

"Don't tell me that his mother's the witch," Thor suggested.

"*A witch?*"

"Don't pay any attention to him, Selene."

A boy about thirteen years old wearing tennis shoes and jeans emerged from the house. He was dark complected and had indigenous features.

"Alas!" he exclaimed calling Alaín by his nickname, "did you just arrive?"

"We're going up Tepozteco. Want to join?"

"You bet."

"Great! Let me introduce my Mexico City friends: Yanira, Selene, Indra, Homero, Thor, and you already know Erika."

"Nice to meet you, Pancho," said Thor. "I was just telling the girls that you're handsome."

"You're funny," Pancho answered dryly.

"Well I think he's handsome," Indra said, cool as a cucumber looking him over.

"Let's go," Alaín exclaimed and started running.

They all took off after him, including Erika, who also shouted, "Let's go!"

They headed up, almost running up the stone stairway that had been constructed by the Toltecs many centuries earlier. On one side was a waterfall and on the other the overwhelming greenery. They reached the top out of breath. From there they could see below them the expansive valleys of Tepoztlán, Cuautla and Cuernavaca. In the far off distance, they also could see the mysterious mountain peaks of Chalcatzingo as well as the curvature of the Earth. The kids were delighted. Then they climbed the Toltec pyramid that was located there and from the top could see behind them Mount Ajusco, which now did not seem so high. They stopped to buy some sodas at the kiosk of the caretaker of the archeological zone. Pancho told them that the caretaker would climb up and down every day almost running, even while carrying two and three cases of sodas on his head. That inspired the kids to run back down so fast that it was a miracle they didn't tumble or skid on the stone steps or bang into the stone walls. Once they had returned to the bottom, they felt their legs trembling.

"Holy moly!" Thor announced. "My legs feels like spaghetti."

After that, Pancho took them to the Corredores, where the view was just as splendid, and then they went into a small cave causing some bats to fly out.

"*Ay, mamá!*" Selene screamed as the dark flying mammals rushed out.

"Dracula!" Thor exclaimed.

"Hey, let's get out of here, okay?" Yanira begged.

"Calm down, girls," Alaín said. "If Pancho says there's no danger, then there's no danger."

"Of course, it's safe," Pancho explained. "The bats have already flown off, and this is a tiny cave. You should see the one I discovered a few days ago!"

"Where?" Alaín asked.

"Is it really cool?" asked Thor.

"It's really neat! Gigantic! You have to bring flashlights because it's super dark. Believe me, it's a really BIG cavern, just like the one at Cacahuamilpa!"

"Oh, come on, don't exaggerate," Erika said.

"So, where's that cave supposed to be?" Homero inquired.

"It's higher up the mountain. You go up this way but then take a turn off that nobody is aware of—I've actually asked people and nobody is familiar with that humongous cavern."

"So, what's the deal?" Selene asked. "Is it scary?"

"Well, maybe a little, yes? But we'll go as a group, and I can take along my machete."

"Darn!" Thor exclaimed. "I wish I had brought my father's rifle! It's like the Terminator's, with a laser scope and everything—we love it!"

"Take it easy, man, who do you think you are, Rambo?"

"Right, he's Thor the Barbarian."

"No, he's just a barbarian."

"But, it isn't dangerous, is it?" insisted Yanira.

"No way, what makes you think that? It's just dark, and we'll take lanterns or flashlights."

"My dad has a big, powerful lantern. Maybe he'll lend it to us," Alaín offered.

"Okay, then, let's go," Homero said.

"No, not today," Pancho interrupted. "It'll soon get dark. We can do it tomorrow . . . we can leave after breakfast and go until supper time."

"We can take some food and have a picnic," Erika proposed enthusiastically.

"Yeah, some sandwiches," Yanira agreed.

"Yes, let's do it!" Selene blurted out.

"So, you want to come too?" Thor asked.

"Yes, even if it is a little scary," she answered.

"Don't worry, I'll take care of you," Thor promised.

"Then we all agree," Alaín announced.

"We're on for tomorrow," Erika confirmed.

❖❖❖

They hurried down narrow Aniceto Villamar Street and when they got home, they found out that Alaín's mother had to spend some time with Pancho's mother because her cleansing had not been finished the previous night. This pricked the ears of all the kids. Alaín, feeling smug, explained some things about the cleansings, and about the male and female witches in Tepoztlán. Erika was the most impressed and requested that she too be given a cleansing.

"Why would you need to be cleansed?" Coral commented. "You're young, you're already clean for sure, no?"

"I'm not sure but I want one. Please, ma'am, take me with you and I promise I won't bother you."

"She doesn't need a cleansing, all she needs is a bath," Homero laughed.

"Very funny. . . ."

"I'd like to go, too," Yanira said.

"Me, too," said everyone else, including Selene.

"I can't take everyone."

"Sure you can," Pancho contradicted, "just as long as they're quiet."

"Oh, yeah, I'll be quiet, like a dead person, but I want to see the witch."

"Look, sweetie, don't expect to see the witch from "Snow White." Just the opposite, she's a very good person, she's really a *healer*, like a doctor but with alternative methods. So, okay, I'll take you all with me, but if Mrs. Guillermina says you have to leave, then you immediately leave. She lives close by."

"Agreed," Homero said.

"Okay, then, let's go," Erika said. "I'm so excited."

"Do you really want to have a cleansing done?"

"Yes, what's wrong with that?"

"I want one too," Homero said. "Let's see if the Turbo Llorona ghost appears in her nightgown."

"Can we eat supper first?" Selene asked.

It was already eight-thirty and they hadn't eaten, they had operated on all cylinders all afternoon.

"No, we'll eat later," Coral said, leading the group out.

Everyone followed her. Once again, they went down the narrow Aniceto Villamar Street to the bridge, which was deserted and poorly lit. All they could see was a group of Indians wearing sombreros, quietly drinking beers in front of a large tent. They turned a corner and came to a house that had no windows and only a door facing the street. The door led to an interior patio that extended to a stable and chicken coops.

Alaín lowered his voice, maybe because of being in the shadows, and said that at one side of the house there was a *temazcal*, a type of sauna used by the Aztecs, where Pancho's family bathed in water heated by burning fragrant logs. But the family was on the other side of the house, where Pancho's mother was accompanied by two Indian women.

Pancho's mother, Señora Guillermina, was a young looking forty-year-old with dark skin and fine facial features. She had a *rebozo* shawl covering her head as she stood in front of an altar with statues of the Virgin of Guadalupe, Jesus Christ wearing the crown of thorns, prints of saints and religious and mystical symbols amid six medium-sized candles and flowers. At the back of the room, in the shadows, there were some beds.

"What's that smell?" Selene asked, her eyes wide open.

Behind her, Alaín's mother stood by the altar speaking in a hushed voice to Señora Guillermina.

"It's *copal*, Mexican incense," answered Alaín. "Do you like it?"

"Yes . . . I think so."

"I prefer this incense to the ones they sell in packets," Alaín added, "'cause those others are too perfumy."

"Good evening, children," Señora Guillermina greeted them without moving toward them.

"Good evening," some of the kids responded quietly.

Why are we speaking in hushed voices, Erika asked herself. She wanted to know about everything that was happening. The incense, the candles and the dim lighting made her feel she was having an enchanting dream.

Coral was standing in the middle of a circle with an Indian woman drawn on the floor. At least, it looked like a woman.

Señora Guillermina stopped praying in front of the altar, picked up some green branches with tiny leaves, dipped them into the liquid of a clay pot and then went around and tapped them on Coral's face, neck, torso, back, belly, arms, legs and feet. Señora Guillermina was completely focused on this exercise.

Next, she rubbed an egg all over Coral's body while whispering some chants, and then repeated the operation with two more eggs, after which she cracked the eggs, and Erika saw that the yokes and whites of the eggs had turned into a black, ugly mass with some clots and sticky parts. They smelled awful.

"Yuck," Selene uttered.

With a slight gesture, Señora Guillermina signaled for Pancho to get rid of the rotten eggs.

Erika was stunned and her heart was pounding because Señora Guillermina had picked up a very fine white cloth and passed it over Coral's face in the act of cleansing; as she cleaned her face, the cloth turned red and drops of blood and blood clots dripped from it.

"No way!" Thor murmured.

"But how . . . ?" Selene whispered.

"Shhh," Indra scolded her with a gaping mouth.

Erika was fixated, feeling the silence like something dense, tense, alive, mysterious, dangerous, a living thing . . . The other kids stared, impressed by the shadows, the odor of incense and the healer's rituals.

Señora Guillermina was in a trance-like state, breathing heavily. A very serious-looking Coral seemed not to react, as the healer passed some cloths over her arms and legs that became soaked in blood and started dripping. She then sprinkled Coral's body with the fragrant water from the branches that had been dipped in the clay pot. She ended by praying something like a litany and handing Coral a jar with tea from a small clay pot.

Coral willingly took small sips, still feeling the calming effects of the cleansing but then almost dropped the jar on hearing Erika cry out to the surprise of all, "I want to go next, please! Whatever it takes!"

"Cool it," Alaín whispered, as he stood next to her.

"Leave me alone. . . . I'm next, Señora. Me! Me!" Erika insisted, almost sobbing.

"Stop screeching, Erika," Indra ordered.

"Oh, Erika," Yanira added.

"But I want to, you hear me?"

Coral looked at Señora Guillermina, who was shaking her head no.

"Some other day, girl," Coral told Erika. "Today, she was only prepared for my cleansing. Besides, we had all agreed to keep quiet and, if Señora Guillermina says no, it means NO."

"Think it over carefully," Señora Guillermina said, "and don't get carried away. Tomorrow night, if you still want a cleansing and *need* one, I'll cleanse you, but understand: this is not a game. This is carried out when God decides there is a need."

"Yes, yes, I want it!"

"Tomorrow, we'll see," Coral said, in a matter-of-fact tone.

❖❖❖

That night, the kids were very excited. Pancho stayed to spend the night with them, "to go hike the mountain very early." First in the back yard and later by the swimming pool, the kids discussed the cleansing that had really impressed them. After that, they played cards until they got bored and started asking "indiscrete questions," almost arguing, and they decided to make some popcorn and stream some movies from the internet satellite dish. They barely understood what they were watching, except for Homer and Alaín, because the movies didn't have Spanish subtitles. Besides, they kept fighting over the remote control and changing channels.

Finally, they gave up, and the boys went to their rooms to play some video games, and the girls went to their rooms to laugh and giggle loudly.

"Shut up, already!" Alaín's father had to scream out.

II

"Are you sure this is the path?" Alaín asked, because it didn't really look like a path, and there was no option other than to follow Pancho, who was forging ahead by pushing plants and branches out of the way.

"Yes, of course," Pancho responded. "I just got back from here, and I marked the path."

"But during the rainy season, all your markings mean nothing."

"I left marks that won't get erased," Pancho insisted. He stopped, examined the giant walls of Mount Tepozteco and saw some kind of indication, because he continued to march upward. They had left Alaín's house at eight that morning with lanterns, food and a machete. They headed up the Tepozteco mountain range first through a short arid hill that was dusty and steep. It soon brought them to dense vegetation overgrowing the paths. They climbed upward without much difficulty until they got to Corredores and the small cave from the previous day. From there, they had to cross a very narrow trail along a mountain cliff. They had not reached very high yet, but at that point the altitude was enough to impress them all, especially the kids from the city, who had a hard time making it through mountain forests. They were pretty meek, thought Pancho.

Alaín was the most adept of them, moving with ease, but of course that was no surprise because he had spent at least four months of each year in Tepoztlán since he was little.

Next best after Alaín was . . . Erika! She was great in the wild, easily climbing up peaks, climbing up trees—she really was. In time she could become an expert. Indra, on the other hand, was the worst, always falling behind and bothering Pancho, looking at him in a way no one had ever looked at him.

The rest had a hard time moving forward and at times they had to be helped, especially when they had to cross the rushing *arroyos* on slippery rocks. Pancho had a good laugh the first time they had to cross one, when chubby Thor crossed over it on all fours and got soaked.

"Don't laugh," Alaín had said, "'cause someday he'll be laughing at you when you lose your way in Mexico City."

After climbing for a long way, they came upon a wide-open space, where they could see the town of Tepoztlán down below and to the right. At first the city dwellers had been gabbing and gabbing, laughing and laughing, and Erika was trying to show everyone the way to go. Then, they started singing their bawdy song again, "from the front and from behind," but by the time they had reached this altitude, they were moving along very quietly, exhausted, through the thick undergrowth and across the more frequent rushing streams that emerged from waterfalls. As they traversed cliffs, the panoramic view lifted their spirits, even as the sky towards the Popocatépetl volcano in the distance was filling with threatening clouds.

"Are we there yet?" Selene kept asking.

It was Selene who convinced Erika to give out the snacks, including potato chips, fruits and a great trail mix made up of peanuts, raisins and M&Ms that Alaín's mother had prepared so they would "have enough calories" for the climb.

"Hey, Pancho, if you had told me that we'd be climbing so much, I wouldn't have come," said Indra after devouring a donut.

"Me neither," Yanira agreed.

"You two are really soft," Erika challenged. "It's been tough but enjoyable."

"My little feet are shaking," cried Selene.

"Mine were already shaking when we went back down yesterday," Indra added.

Then, everyone remembered that their feet had trembled, or that their calves and ankles had vibrated after their running descent from Tepozteco.

"It felt really good," Thor commented.

"We're really close now," Pancho informed them.

And they were. At the next bend, they arrived at what looked like a slit in Tepozteco's walls.

"This is it!" Pancho announced. "Look, here's my mark," he said pointing above the cut in the rock face, where lines on the cliff formed a serpent biting its tail.

It was kind of blurred, but on close inspection, one could see and appreciate a possible Toltec style in the engraving, if that's what it was, and not a natural formation in the sone, like so many others.

"It's a snake eating its tail!" Homero exclaimed on seeing it.

"And it is covered in feathers," Pancho added. "Let's go in."

They entered through the slit, which little by little widened into what looked like a cave, but soon they saw something light up ahead. The grotto narrowed again and soon led outside to a small clearing covered in vegetation.

"We're here!" announced Pancho, all excited. "The entrance is straight ahead . . . this is only the doorway."

This, plus the suspense of passing through the slit and of course having snacked, lifted their spirits, and they crossed through energetically with the hefty use of the machete. They soon arrived at the other side, where they found a cavity in the stone wall, through which they could only go on all fours.

"Through there?!" Indra complained.

"Man, how were you able to find this hole?" Thor asked, not believing his eyes.

"Just by accident . . . after I had discovered the serpent out front. It was just after a landslide, when there were a lot of rocks strewn around . . . and, I guess, that's how the serpent drawing came to light. If not for that, someone would have discovered it earlier. Here in Tepoztlán, there are many people who know the Tepozteco mountain range better than I do. So that serpent must have been hidden by this very mountain, and just as we see it uncovered, it must have gotten covered way back."

"Neat," Thor commented, very impressed.

"Yeah, really neat," Homero agreed.

"So then, I went in through the slit and found this place, and since then I've come here often . . .'cause I just feel good here, and then just a few days ago, I found that little opening. It was strange that I hadn't seen it before because, if you look closely, it's pretty much in the open. So, well, then I went in and realized it was very dark in there and so the next time I brought a flashlight."

"And what did you see?"

"Oh, let him tell us later. We can go in now and see for ourselves," Alaín said.

"Yes," Erika agreed. "Less talk and more action. I'm going in first!" she added, and with that she pushed through the small entrance. "A flashlight, please!" she called out.

"Man, she's something else!" exclaimed Pancho.

Alaín passed her the flashlight and ordered, "Get going, everyone."

One by one, they all went through the hole and emerged in what seemed to be a small cave, like the previous one. But this time it was a real cave and, after running through it a bit, it seemed very long. They came upon two openings that appeared to go off in different directions.

Erika stopped short. "Which way?" she asked.

"Now you ask?" said Alaín. "Weren't you leading the way?"

"I'm gonna stay in the lead as soon as buddy here says which way."

"Hmm, I can't remember . . ." Pancho mumbled.

"What do you mean?!"

"But I do remember that there were tunnels that took me to a giant cavern with a very high ceiling. I looked around for a long time and saw that at the other end were some other tunnel entrances, so I decided to go back."

"Booooring," Erika said. "So, it looks like you don't know which way. . . . So, I'm gonna take the lead. Let's go this way," she said, most confidently, as she went into the tunnel on the left.

"Hold on, whoa," Alaín exclaimed.

"What's up?"

"This is a very important decision. Let's see what everyone thinks."

"Come on already! Let's see."

"Which way should we go?" Alaín asked. "Down the left tunnel or the right one?"

"I'll go either way . . . how about the left?" Indra said. "But the truth is, I'm getting pretty tired. . . ."

"Take it easy, girl," Alaín said. "That's all right."

"I say that way," Homero said, pointing to the right.

"Oh, yeah, just to contradict me, huh?" Erika said.

"No, not really," countered Homero.

"So why not?"

"Just no."

"This guy's mental," Pancho laughed.

Yanira voted for the left and Alaín for the right. So the four girls chose the left. Pancho had to break the tie and said without thinking, "The left one."

"Man, that was not cool. You took the girls' side," Homero accused him.

"Not really. It's that I'm pretty sure now that it was down the left tunnel."

And that's where they went. The lanterns lit up the humid earthen walls studded with stones, although most of the walls in the tunnel were of pure rock. What series of accidents, Alaín wondered, could have formed the tunnels, or even worse, what kind of humans could have created them. The Toltecs, obviously. But it was such a great feat of underground engineering, how could the Toltecs have managed it? They came upon the opening of another tunnel, and again Pancho led the way. And further down, they found another tunnel, and then another, and another, and another.

"Phew! I hope we don't get lost. . . ." Alaín said.

"We're just going around and around in circles," Erika added, somewhat worried. "Are you sure that it's this way?"

"I'm pretty sure," Pancho answered, "but, one hundred percent . . . not really."

"It all looks the same," Thor said.

"Did you mark the trail?" Alaín asked.

"Marked?"

"You gotta be kidding!"

"Are we lost?" Selene asked.

"No, uh-uh," Pancho answered as he turned into another tunnel that looked identical to the previous ones.

"Oh, brother, this is so creepy," whispered Yanira.

"Everything's so quiet," Erika commented.

And then, they reached the cavern. It was as immense as Pancho had said. Sounds were magnified by a strong echo and vibration. Pancho whistled, and the sound became metallic, rebounding off the walls, becoming distorted and then silenced. The lanterns were strong enough to shed light on some strange stone formations: stalactites and stalagmites that were shining from the condensed humidity. The overall sensation in the cavern was of vastness and magnificence.

"This is the place I told you about."

"You were right. It's gigantic," Alaín replied.

"Yes, and you can't see where it ends."

"It seems like a dream," Selene added.

"It's like the Cacahuamilpa caves, but in the dark," Thor offered.

"It's kind of cold down here, no?" Indra said.

"It's cool, all right," Homero commented.

"It's sensational," Yanira insisted.

"Doesn't it seem strange?" Erika said.

"Like, how?"

"Like . . ." Erika said as she turned a full circle, ". . . Like there's light. Turn off the lanterns!"

Alaín, Pancho and Indra turned them off, and suddenly they were plunged into an absolute darkness that forced them to grab onto each other. The silence was so complete that all they could hear was the rapid beating of their hearts. But after a few moments, they were able to distinguish a faint brightness at one end of the giant cave.

"What's that?" Erika whispered.

"What?" Thor asked.

"It's like a light."

"Well, then it's a light."

"Stop joking around."

"Me?" Thor said. "It's . . . I don't know what it is."

"Anyway, I wasn't even talking to you."

"Is it a light or not?" interjected Alaín.

"But, how can there be light in a cavern?" Homero asked.

"Who knows? . . . It could be an opening to the outside," Alaín guessed.

"Or someone's there," Selene suggested.

"No way," murmured Indra.

"I see it . . . something . . ." Yanira said

"I don't see a thing," Thor asserted.

"What do we do?"

"Let's go see it," Pancho said pointing.

And then there was an absolute silence again that made the rest of them nervous.

"It's the worst thing you could do," announced a voice that did not belong to any of them.

"Who said that?" Pancho said and turned on his lantern.

The kids blinked in surprise and looked around.

"What do you mean, who?" Thor asked.

"Yeah, who said, 'It's the worst thing you can do'?"

". . . could do," Alaín corrected him.

"Well, who said it?" Pancho asked hesitantly.

"Not me," said Selene.

"Or any of us . . ." Alaín said quietly.

They turned three hundred and sixty degrees with their light beams without seeing anything in the silence of the cavern.

"We're screwed. Now, we're seeing things," Thor said.

"Hearing things. Hallucinations," Alaín corrected him.

"And what does that mean?" Selene asked.

"Whatever . . ." Homero responded.

"Oh, I give up . . ." Selene countered.

"This is no joking matter," Indra reproached them.

"What did that voice sound like?" Pancho asked.

"Strong, young, in command," Erika answered.

"No, it was an old man's and like . . . chanted," Indra said.

"Yes, it was like an old man's but horrific, like from beyond the grave, I'm not sure, like it was hoarse . . . I don't know, bloody. Horrible!" Yanira added her opinion.

"Yeah, it sounded like an old man to me too, but like it wasn't serious, tricky . . . although somewhat evil, ugh!" Thor recounted.

"How about you, Alaín?" Homero asked.

"For me, it was like it came from the center of the Earth. It was deafening but quiet at the same time, and it could be heard very clearly. . . . How about you, Homero?"

"How about me?" Selene complained. "You guys always ask me last and don't pay any attention to me . . . just because I'm the youngest."

"You're right, short stuff. Tell us what you thought," said Thor.

"Okay, that's your contribution to children's liberation," Homero said sarcastically. "Free thee smalle-e-e peopol-l-l-l-l."

Selene proceeded: "I heard it very clearly. It was like a kid's voice, like a leader of children, a kid boss . . . a Child King!" Selene summarized.

"Holy smoke! She really got into it," Thor commented.

"It sounded soft, serious, velvety to me," Homero said.

"How is that possible? We all heard something different!"

"But no one heard a woman's voice," Erika said.

"The feminist has spoken," Homero spit out.

"Hey, it's okay to be a feminist," Yanira said.

"What do you know?"

"How about you, Pancho, what did it sound like to you?" Indra asked.

They suddenly realized that they had forgotten about Pancho, much to their embarrassment.

"I heard it with my whole body. It was like all of my muscles were feeling a presence that was impossible to ignore. It was something powerful and strange, also like something I was familiar with from way back . . ."

"Jeez!" Thor exclaimed.

"Of course, you know me well, Panchito," the voice was heard saying. It was coming from everywhere.

At that, they all jumped, startled.

"I know you?" muttered Pancho, pale, almost trembling.

They were all wary, maintaining absolute silence, until a giggle could be heard emerging from different parts of the cave at the same time.

"My God, what is that?!" Erika screamed. "Who *is* that?"

"Now, he's laughing at us," Alaín whispered as the giggling grew louder.

"Who are you?" insisted Erika.

"I am your father, Tezca," the voice said.

"Let's get out of here," said Yanira, overwhelmed by fear. "We're going crazy."

"Don't leave, kids," the voice said. "Why don't we play a game of war, everyone against everyone else, with no time limit, conquer or die!"

Homero laughed at the combative tone of the last phrase, but then realized that he suddenly felt a deep, heated hate for everyone present, for those ridiculous kids he had to put up with during the whole trip! He needed to punish them, hard, severely! To cut out their hearts so they'd learn a lesson! Yes, that's it: cut out their hearts!

Homero was shaking with hate, and in his fury he noticed that all of them were feeling the same thing, hearing the laughter that was coming from everywhere, looking at each other with savage hate, mortal, insufferable expectation . . .

Selene suddenly ran and gave Homero a powerful kick in the shins.

"Darn it!!!" she yelled and spit three times at the ground in front of him. He could not keep himself from grabbing Selene violently and raising his fist to strike her with all his might.

"Hit her! I've had enough of her!" Indra screamed.

"Yeah, get her!" Yanira yelled.

"And I'm gonna kill you," Thor shouted. "I'm gonna kill you all!"

"Okay, you've played your usual tricks. Now, leave us alone!" Pancho ordered in a commanding voice, full of authority and leaving them all paralyzed. "Your giggling ends right NOW!" he added, holding up his hands in a strange gesture. "Kids, for the love of God," he added in his usual voice, "calm down. Everyone, calm down. You, Homero, let her go. Let her go!"

Homero let Selene go, and she broke into tears. Erika went to her and hugged her.

"What happened, Erika, what happened?" Selene asked.

"I don't know. It all happened so fast. . . ."

The eight kids looked at each other and just then realized that the giggling and laughter had ceased. What had seemed to exist was no longer there. It all had happened in a flash. They were astonished and looked at each other without understanding what had happened.

"Well," Alaín said, "Selene was right. What just happened?"

"I don't know," said Thor. "I was my usual self, right? . . . And then I suddenly felt something . . . something weird, like anger . . . I felt like avenging myself . . ."

"Taking vengeance? On whom?"

"Me too, I felt really angry," Selene exclaimed. "Ugh! It was ugly, *ugly*!"

It became obvious that they had all felt the same overwhelming hate at the same time.

"It was all because . . ." Erika guessed, "that lousy voice told us to play war. . . ."

"Yes, that was it!" Alaín agreed. "Remember? We were to fight against each other to the *death*."

"And then," Yanira added, "how did it stop?"

"Pancho did it," Homero answered.

"That's right," Erika said, thoughtfully.

They all turned to Pancho, who was very quiet, pensive.

"How did you do it, Pancho? What was it you told him?" Alaín asked.

"I . . . I . . . don't know. All of a sudden, I felt a deep, very strong force in me. It was so strong, that I could not hold back. . . . I don't remember what I said, but it was like I was riding a giant wave, the strongest wave, and then I realized that the laughter had disappeared."

"The laughter, right?" Thor said. "But, how did you do it?"

"I'm telling you, I don't know, but it's like I'm always about to remember *something* . . . And my head hurts . . . like I'm in a trance . . . It happens to me now and then."

"There's something *very* strange here," Alaín declared.

Everyone became silent when they heard what sounded like a noise close by. Everyone sharpened their hearing as best they could for some moments that seemed eternal. And, then, far off, from the place where the brightness seemed to be, someone was approaching.

"What's that?" Erika asked.

"Oh, my God," murmured Indra.

"Erika," Selene said as she grabbed onto her.

"It's an old man," Homero said.

"It's a little old Indian man," Alaín specified.

In fact, it was, and he was getting closer fast, taking large hops toward them.

"He must be drunk," Erika said.

Indra nervously shined her light on the old man, who seemed to shrink from the light and grumbled something in a strange language.

"He says not to shine the light in his face," Pancho instructed.

"How do you know what he says?" Indra asked.

"Because I speak Nahuatl. Don't shine the light on him, Indra."

"*Nahuatl?*" Indra repeated. "You speak Nahuatl?" she said as she turned the light away.

The old man was very close now. He was, indeed, a very old Indian, very dark with completely white hair. He wore a palm-frond hat, and his clothes were wrinkled and dirty. He was carrying a clay bottle, and his entire body reeked of alcohol.

"I'm really scared," Selene whispered.

"And why are you scared, little girl? I'm not that ugly, huh? C'mon, tell me, am I that ghastly looking, or what?"

"No, sir," Selene said, looking him mover carefully, astonished that she no longer felt afraid.

"What are you kids doing here?"

"We were just walking around," Alaín answered, "and we discovered the entrance to this cave and we came in to explore it."

"But you didn't ask for permission, did you?" the old man growled in complaint.

"But permission from whom?" Erika interjected.

"From me, who else?"

"But we didn't know we had to ask for permission," Erika argued.

"Well, now you know!" he told her and, just like that, he took a large swig from his bottle, after which he issued a loud, stinky "Ahhhhh!"

"Okay, will you give us permission to walk around in this cave, mister?" Alaín asked politely.

"Only if you have a drink with me," the old man answered, lifting up his bottle. "You first, little girl," he said, looking at Selene as he sat down on a large stone.

"Not me, what!!!"

"Listen, sir, she's a little kid, she can't be drinking," Thor protested.

"Oh, fiddlesticks, why not? This here drink is medicinal. With a little more protein it would be meat—everyone knows that. It cures everything that ails you."

"Well, what is that stuff?" asked Homero, interested now.

"Okay, this guy's gonna have a few swigs with me!" exclaimed the old man, laughing slyly.

"Homero, NO!" Yanira yelled.

"Oh, no, I was just asking . . ." Homero explained.

"This? It's pure life. It's a white liquor that a little friend of mine, who has my same name, squeezes out of the maguey cactus. It's called *téumetl.*"

"*Téumetl*," Erika repeated. "As far as I'm concerned, it's *pulque* alcohol."

"So, do you want a drink or not? You have to drink with me and get really drunk, or I won't give you permission to come into my home!" he reasoned.

"We're underage, if we go home stinking of booze, we'll really be in trouble."

"But if you don't drink with me," the old man said, laughing, "you'll never get out of here."

"That's not true, right, Yanira?" Selene asked.

"No, sweetie."

"Think about it, kids, while I compose a poem," he said and staggered away behind a big boulder.

Soon, the kids heard a powerful stream of urine followed by a loud "Ahhhhh!"

They looked at each other. They didn't know what to do, but for some reason, they weren't afraid at all. A couple of them were even smiling. Only Pancho remained very wary.

And then, it was not the old drunk who returned from behind the boulder but a skinny, black, hairless dog. He started growling when they shined their flashlights and lanterns on him. They all held their breath as the dog started towards Thor and sniffed his jeans and tennis shoes, and just like that raised his leg and pissed on his legs.

"Damn dog, he pissed on me! Yuck!" Thor protested furiously and tried to kick the dog.

"That's an Aztec dog . . ." Alaín began to explain as the dog ran off and disappeared in the darkness.

And the old man was nowhere to be seen. The kids looked at each other, surprised.

"This is really weird," Alaín said.

"Screwy, I'd say," Thor said.

"Erika, can you share some of your snacks?" whispered Selene nervously, her eyes as big as saucers.

"Here, take the whole bag," Erika said without paying much attention.

Selene grabbed them and pushed a handful of chips into her mouth. Just then, Erika realized what she'd done and grabbed the bag back, but Selene could not complain with her mouth full.

The kids proceeded in the direction the dog had run off, but they didn't see anything. Everywhere they shined their lights they saw humid rock formations or an endlessly dense darkness. Just then, a little light seemed to emit from behind some large square boulders. And just as suddenly, they got a

whiff of tortillas. They took off in that direction and were surprised to see that the rocks had taken the shape of a house,
with a roof and an entrance. Out in front there was an elegant,
pretty Indian woman with her back to them making tortillas.
She was squatting in the center of a stone platform raised
about two feet high, where she was placing flat, round tortilla
dough on a clay *comal*, heated by the flames rising from
stones formed into a brasier. The light surrounding her was
reddish and warm. The tortillas smelled delicious.

That's when the kids immediately felt hungry and in great
need of rest. They looked at each other, afraid to speak to the
woman. Nevertheless, after a bit, with her back to them but
somehow looking at them, they heard her say: "C'mon, kids,
have a seat."

Thor and Selene were the first to approach the woman.
They looked her over carefully. Then, Erika, Alaín, Indra,
Yanira, Homero and Pancho followed.

She was taking the dough balls she had prepared, softly
flattened them between her palms, delicately shaping them
into tortillas, and placed them elegantly on the *comal*, and
turning over some that were already there cooking and remov-
ing the others that were done. She placed them in a straw
basket, which was on a doily embroidered with the words "I
love you." Next to the *comal* there were clay pots and pans
filled with a variety of stews. But more impressive than these
was the woman herself, who overwhelmed them with a
strange emotion. She dressed in a very elegant, dark *huipil*
that sparkled all over like stars in the night sky. A white shawl
covered her head like snow on a mountain. It was impossible
to tell her age, but she was simply beautiful, with fine facial
features and a serene and majestic composure. In her presence, they felt like lying down and being pampered, to feel

warm while drinking hot chocolate and be told a story while outside a storm was brewing.

"Let's see, who wants some? There's stewed *nopal* cactus with cheese and radishes, tender squash with armadillo meat, turkey in *mole* sauce, quail in *pipián* sauce, corn on the cob and beans. To drink, I have *chía* water.

The kids looked at each other in shock. They realized how happy they felt, and they felt like laughing, but only smiled timidly because the woman's presence was so imposing.

"Yes, thank you," Erika said.

"You are welcome, young lady, but what do you all want to eat?"

"Oh, I want the *mole*," Selene said.

"Me, too," Erika exclaimed.

"I'd like the *nopalitos* and quail," Indra joined in.

"Can I have the stewed squash with . . . what? Armadillo meat? What's that taste like?" Alaín asked.

"Oh, it tastes really good," Pancho said.

"He knows what he's talking about. Pay attention to him," the lady said as she was placing tortillas on clay plates, spooning the stews into them and passing the plates to the kids, all of whom were crowding around the brasier.

"I'd like a plate of everything, Señora," Thor specified, already licking his chops.

"No class, Thor, already taking advantage," Homero criticized.

"Missus, you sure are a great cook," Selene said.

"Oh, yeah," Indra agreed.

"And to think, I was so scared," Selene said, wistfully.

"What were you afraid of, sweetie?" the lady asked as she continued to serve the food.

"Uh, I'm not sure . . . *of everything* . . . . but especially of that crazy old man we ran into."

"Here you go," the lady said, and then asked, "Tell me, what old man are you talking about?"

"It was a drunk old guy," Yanira said. "Can you believe it, Señora? He wanted to get us drunk!"

The lady laughed as she served the plates to the background of the kids commenting: "How scrumptious!" "This is so delicious." "Man, you've got to taste this armadillo, it's super-tasty."

"Oh, I know who you're talking about. Don't mind him," the lady said. "You, dear, what would you like?"

"A little *mole*, please," answered Yanira.

"So, who is he?" Alaín asked between bites.

"I'd like some armadillo with baby squash, and also some *nopales*," Homero put in his request.

"And to think, we brought sandwiches," Selene laughed. "This is a lot better."

"Yes, they brought their sandwiches," Pancho told the lady.

"So, who was he?" Alaín repeated with his mouth full.

"You, what would you like, sonny?" she asked Pancho.

"Me? Armadillo!"

"Oh, I want to try the armadillo, too," Selene said.

"Little one, how can you eat so much?!" Yanira commented.

"Me, too. I'd like to try the 'dillo," Erika added.

"Who . . . who was that guy, darn it?" Alaín insisted.

"Who's who?" Indra asked.

"The old drunk guy."

"Oh, he's just some jokester who's always going around trying to trick everybody. He says it's just for laughs," the lady explained.

"But, what's his name?"

"Here, we call him Tezca, or Titla," she answered with a sweet smile as she watched the kids devour their tacos. *Poor things*, she must have been thinking, *they were dying of hunger*.

"Yes, that's what he said his name was," Homero agreed.

"What is this place?" Alaín asked. "Where do you all live?"

"Well, here," said the lady, looking at Alaín sweetly.

And Alaín immediately was overcome by a sense of peace and gratitude for being there.

"And what does he do? I mean the old drunk?"

"I'm guessing that you'll soon find out. . . . You'll see for yourselves all that he is capable of doing."

"Señora," Thor interrupted, "can you serve me a little more?"

The lady agreed, picked up a plate and served him some more. Everyone kept eating ravenously but in silence. A great sense of peace had settled over them all, so that all they had to do was eat and quietly enjoy their food. . . . Soon, Selene, pushed her plate aside and looked at the lady, who was smiling at her.

"Oh, Señora," she said, "thank you so much. It was delicious. I think I must have been really hungry, 'cause, believe me, I feel a lot stronger now."

"Oh, it's just that you're a bottomless pit," Erika said. "Would you like some more?"

"No, I'm full," the girl answered and lay down at the edge of the lady's *huipil*. "What is your name?"

"Tona."

"Whoa," exclaimed Erika, "what rude people we are. We haven't told the Señora anything, not even our names."

"No worries, I already know who you all are," she said with a smile. "You are Erika, you Alaín, you Yanira, you Indra . . . and Homero . . . your name is Selene, and this beautiful boy goes by Pancho."

"He doesn't just go by it," specified Alaín. "His name *is* Pancho."

Tona looked questioningly at Alaín, who immediately experienced a strange sensation, as if he comprehended that there were so many things he didn't know. And it filled him with a deep desire to learn as much as possible as well as shame for always acting like he knew everything. He also realized that Pancho seemed to be suspended in the air.

"Okay, and who are all these children," a female voice said, startling them.

"Ah, Chico, you've arrived," Tona greeted a thin elderly but energetic woman, also dark-skinned and wearing a beautiful red huipil. On her head she sported a diadem as a crown and had a glass of water in her hand.

"These children discovered the entrance."

"That can't be."

"Oh, yes, it can, and you know it full well. Here they are, as you can see," Tona said, because Chico had been looking only at Tona and at no time had looked at the kids.

"Should I look at them?"

"Yes, look."

"And do the others know?"

"What questions, Chico!"

"Well, it's because all this really does not interest me. . . . I've got too many things to do to be involved in everything here. Let the others find out for themselves."

"Now, Chico, are you going to look at them or not?"

"Chico sighed and finally faced the kids, who had been observing dumbfounded while the women conversed as if they weren't there. Even Thor was frozen with a *nopales* taco in his hand.

Chico took a few steps in their direction, spinning the glass she held. She was looking over the kids with a dubious smile until she came to Pancho and looked surprised. He, on the other hand, felt as if he knew this woman despite not ever having met her in his life. She noticed that he was looking directly into her eyes and that there was a very strong link between them both. Pancho was feeling like something within him was being settled and that soon he would learn something very important. But it was very annoying to feel that he was about to remember something and not be able to concentrate on it.

"She is Chico," Tona said to the kids, pointing to the woman who was staring at Pancho.

"You have a lot of nerve returning here after all that happened," she scolded.

"Me?" asked Pancho, bewildered.

"Yes, you. Don't play innocent. I hope you intend to do what you promised."

"But I've never seen you in my life, ma'am. . . ."

"You like to play games"

"Chico, enough already," Tona begged.

"It's that it's coming true, Tona!" Chico exclaimed.

"That's right."

"Well, I don't know . . ." Chico answered, once again insisting energetically. "I do what I'm supposed to, nothing more. And that's plenty. Tona, already in storage are the cartons of eggs, the seafood, the meat . . . there's venison, iguana, frogs, quails, pheasants, grasshoppers, everything, and the greens and the spices. Nothing is missing. If you see Tema, tell her that I've brought all the herbs and rubs she asked for. You can't imagine how difficult she is, Tona. And you too," she added on the way out, pausing to go to Pancho and caress his cheek. "Look, it really doesn't matter to me, but you know how things are . . . Let's see how it turns out this time . . ." she said followed by a sigh.

After that, she left, opening a kind of door through the rocks. "There's no light here," she said, waving her hand softly, and instantly, a dim light appeared and what seemed to be pure rock face became a corridor painted cream color with stylized flowers and decorative lines.

"I guess I should introduce you to the others," Tona said to the kids. "Follow me."

"Right now?" Yanira asked. "We're so comfortable here. . . ."

"Yes, let's go now."

"Selene fell asleep," Erika informed her.

In fact, the little girl had fallen asleep by the stone platform where Tona had been cooking the tortillas.

"It's that she ate like a pig," Thor said.

"Look who's talking."

"Poor thing," Tona mumbled. "Let her rest. I'll leave her my little firefly to follow and find us when she awakes."

"I think it's better to wake her up," Erika insisted. "She'll miss everything."

"No," Tona replied. "We might encounter the *ciguas*, who scare the heck out of children. They can smell them."

"What do they do to them?"

"Oh, they're just bothersome. They're okay down here, but mind what I say."

"Who are the *ciguas*?" Alaín asked, but quieted down when he saw Tona take out a shiny object from her finely woven satchel.

All the kids came in close, curious to see what she had. "How pretty," they said. "What is it?"

Tona opened her fist to reveal a small firefly that kept changing its beautiful luminescent colors.

"Wow!" they responded, "It's really cool!" "It's gorgeous!" "It's out of this world!" "Can I touch it?"

Tona placed the firefly on Selene's head. "You stay here until this girl wakes up," she ordered, "and then you bring her to us wherever we are."

The bug sparkled as if it was saying, "Yes."

"Okay, everybody, let's go," she ordered and led the group down the corridor with cream-colored walls.

"Will she be okay?" Erika asked.

"Don't be afraid. Nothing will happen to her. Come on."

They all followed Tona, looking back at Selene, sound asleep and with a resplendent firefly on her head. They proceeded down the corridor, where they saw a number of doors with stone-carved frames. Some doors opened to large rooms full of shadows. At one point they heard the sound of water running. First it sounded like a nearby stream, then a waterfall and finally like giant waves crashing on the shore.

"What's that?" Alaín wanted to know.

"Yes, what *is* that?" Erika repeated.

"It sounds like an underground river," Homero suggested.

"An underground sea," Alaín specified.

"No," Tona said, "it's Chalch, who likes to sing."

"To sing?" Alaín asked.

"Chalch?" added Erika.

"Yes," Tona affirmed, "she has a great voice."

The rumble kept getting louder, and the kids gave each other questioning looks, but unlike before, they were more curious than scared in Tona's company. They soon arrived at a great hall decorated with paintings of serpents, eagles and jaguars. At the other side, there was a woman wearing a sky-blue *huipil* with a fringe and prints of little shells. She also wore shell earrings and a jeweled necklace with a large gold medal between her breasts. She didn't seem young or old. And, indeed, she was singing, and her songs sounded like breaking waves.

The kids looked at each other, fascinated. The woman was now raising her arms, and the sound she emitted from her mouth was the crashing of waves, so overpowering that they closed their eyes and felt sea breezes on their faces.

"That's Chalch. Do you like how she sings?" Tona asked.

No one answered, each child having fallen into a sort of trance.

Thor saw himself clearly going down the river rapids crashing into boulders. It was a marvelous delirium.

Erika was swimming among rushing waves, diving into them, body-surfing and then standing on the shore challenging them to wash her away.

Indra felt the sea rising to her feet up on an embankment where she was contemplating the setting sun.

Yanira was fishing from the deck of a large boat in the middle of a wide, placid river.

Homero was able to breathe under water like a fish as he calmy harvested jewels from the seabed. Afterward, he rose to the surface to contemplate an enormous full moon.

Alaín, lastly, found the exact point where the currents of a big river merged into the ocean. To his right there was a flock of herons resting by the shore and to his left there were some vultures casually picking at a burro's cadaver under the resplendent noonday sun.

Pancho, however, felt like he was the water.

"How wonderful that you have returned," he heard the voice of Chalch say. "Let's see if things get better now that you're here. You and I need to talk. Don't go disappearing on me."

Tona observed the kids in their dreamy illusions. Their enchantment ended when Chalch stopped singing and approached them.

"Chalch," Tona said, "these are the children who discovered the entryway."

"Yes," Chalch responded, "I already appeared to them to see how they were."

"And how are we?" Erika asked. "Isn't it true that I need a cleansing?"

"And, where are we?" Alaín asked.

"In Tepozteco's belly. Didn't you know?" Chalch answered.

"How can that be? Not even in my dreams!"

Chalch and Tona broke into laughter.

"Do you want me to pinch you to see if you're dreaming?" Chalch answered as she gave Alaín a rough pinch, and he jumped away from her.

"I'm done! I give up! Time off!" he exclaimed, doubling over.

Everyone had a good laugh. And Chalch slowly backed away from the kids and soon dissolved into the shadows, never to be seen again.

"So whatdya say now?" Homero asked Alaín. "Are we dreaming or what?"

Everyone started laughing again. But the laughter was cut short when they saw approaching what looked like the most horrific apparition in the world. It was a giant woman, fearsome, dressed in dark brown, covered in skulls. She was very tall and heavy-set, very dark, with ringlets of hair and a fierce demeanor.

"Everybody hide!" Tona screamed. "And don't come out until I call you," she added, pointing to the hall they had come out of.

The kids quickly returned, but Alaín, Thor and Erika attempted to peek out as the giant woman was closing in with gigantic steps that echoed in the corridor like a mountain walking.

"Oh, glorious lady, great mother Coatlicue," Tona greeted her. "Where are you going in such a hurry?"

"Look, girl," Coatlicue answered, "you can't fool me. There's something strange going on here. For a while now, I have felt the presence of things I had almost forgotten. Outsiders have trespassed here, I'm sure you are hiding them. Turn them over to me right now so that I can entertain myself and later sacrifice them to my son."

"No, no," Tona, replied gently but firmly. "Dear mother, all that sacrificing ended a long time ago. . . ."

"Not for me it didn't. Give them to me, Tona, or you'll be sorry. It's been a while since you felt the brunt of my ire. Remember: you, too, can feel pain."

"Oh, I feel it much more than others do," she replied, sighing.

"Then do me the favor of turning them over to me right now . . . because if I have to go fetch them myself behind some other door, I'll be upset, and it will be worse for them. Every second that I have to wait will increase the severity of my vengeance."

"Oh great Mother, with all due respect, why don't you go outside and produce a giant earthquake instead, so you won't be so uptight?"

"Tona, how dare you show me a lack of respect," Coatlicue exclaimed.

Then the great Mother made a sign and the earth split wide open at Tona's feet. But instead of falling into the abyss, Tona floated in the air over it.

"Now you'll stay there," Coatlicue said and with another gesture froze Tona in the air.

"With due respect, mother Coatlicue, I don't have time for games," replied Tona.

The kids were terrified, hearing all of this from in back of the door. Then they suddenly became aware that a transparent globe was forming around them, and they all held on as best they could to its invisible walls as the globe ascended with great speed. It went through the cave ceiling and above the entire Mount Tepozteco, flying rapidly over the town of Ajusco and headed for Mexico City with its dense salmon-colored cloud of pollution suspended over it. They flew up so high, up to the edge, where the sky becomes firmament, and stopped. Below them stretched a large segment of the continent, the oceans and numerous clouds, but this was no time to admire the beauty of the Earth below. They noticed that Tona was with them, suspended in the air on the outside of the sphere. And then, the terrorific presence of the great Coatlicue was made known to them.

"Well, who do you think you are?!" roared Coatlicue. "Turn those children over to me now!"

"I'm sorry, Mother," Tonatzin replied patiently, "but they're under my protection."

"Is that right? Well, now you'll see what that's worth!"

The kids felt the bottom of their stomachs react as the sphere took off to soar once again into the blackness of what looked like outer space. They all held on to each other and the transparent walls as best they could, because the sphere was spinning and soaring vertiginously. When they were about to leave the light of Earth's atmosphere and plunge into the vacuum of space, they were able to see Tona, now immense in size, waiting for them at the border. Tona stopped the flight of the sphere with a sharp blow of her forearm and projected it back to Earth again.

The kids had to hold on as best they could as they noticed Coatlicue shooting down toward them like a black streak. She quickly reached them and, with a blow from her enormous arms, sent the sphere back up again. The poor kids were sent tumbling head over heels in the sphere and almost did not notice that they were headed for a cloud formation like a giant perfect circle and that they were just a few meters from its center.

"Mother," they heard Tona say, "during these past few centuries, you've lost your mind!"

Tona had already moved to where the transparent sphere was heading in order to bat it with her elbow into the exact center of the giant cloud circle and through it.

"Oh, Momma!" cried Thor, "These darn dames are playing basketball with us!"

"What do you mean *basketball*?" Homero cried, terrified. "This is the ancient ball game played by the Aztecs, except now up in the clouds!"

"You're such a pair!"

"*Ay, ay*, I'm seasick!" Indra was just able to mutter.

"Me, too!" said Thor, "but I'm enjoying their chatter."

"You're crazy," Yanira yelled at him.

"Oops!" Erika said as Coatlicue hit the sphere again, and once again they were headed for the circular cloud, but this time they did not make it through the center.

"Stop it already, Mother!" Tona pleaded from above. "You're out of practice!"

The kids could see that Coatlicue's face was darkening, looking like the head of a dark, enraged serpent. With a slight movement of her hand, she was able to stop the sphere and direct a black fire to encompass its transparent walls and cover its entire surface. The terrified kids realized that deadly black smoke was about to enter the globe.

"*Ay, ay!*" Yanira screamed. "We're going to suffocate!"

"Look," Alaín said, pointing.

They all smelled an aroma of fragrant flowers begin to surround them and blow away the dark, foul smoke. Tona, now by their side, was softly blowing into the sphere.

"Wow!" exclaimed Thor, fascinated.

"What a delicious aroma!" Indra said.

In the distance, Coatlicue looked more furious than ever, her look alone terrorizing the children. Just then, she pushed off with her gigantic arms and took an incredibly long leap. They lost sight of her in the blackness of space, but she soon flew back with supernatural speed and, before Tona could react, leaped onto the transparent sphere.

The kids felt a thunderous blow over their heads, which sent the globe falling downward, soon to sink back into the Tepozteco. They could clearly, although very briefly, see the massive movement of earth, sand, rocks and boulders as the walls of the mountain opened. And suddenly, they were back in the giant cavern again. The transparent sphere dissolved, smelling as if it had burned up.

"Run, run," they heard Tona's voice urge them as if it were coming from inside their skulls. "Get out of here. I'll catch up with you later!"

They escaped, running as fast as they could, while above them the mountain was shaking. They were able to turn off their lights and run in the dark, sensing that Coatlicue would not see them and catch them that way. It was obvious that the giant female thing was coming after them. However, as they ran, banging into the sides of tunnels, it became evident that the danger had subsided.

"No need to run anymore," Pancho said in a strangely calm and firm tone. "Tonatzin is distracting our Mother." And then, he hesitated, surprised by what he had just said.

"How do you know that?" Alaín asked, even more surprised.

"Yes, how do you know that?" Erika repeated.

"I don't know," Pancho answered, puzzled, "but I do."

Alaín looked deeply into the eyes of Pancho, his great Indian friend from Tepoztlán. He realized that he didn't know him all that well. With everything that happened, so much had changed. He realized that something very strange was happening to Pancho, and he thought that he was on the verge of understanding it, although he couldn't just yet.

Pancho had now become very quiet, as if he were observing something in the atmosphere. "Let's go," he said suddenly and started walking into the darkness of the tunnel.

"It's cold in here," Yanira complained.

"How about Selene?" Erika said almost to herself.

"She's all right," Pancho answered, again in that firm tone, exhibiting authority, which all day long had been emerging and puzzling Alaín as much as Pancho.

"Where are we going, Pancho?" Erika asked.

"Yes," Alaín repeated, "where are we going?"

"This way."

"I can't see anything," Yanira said.

In fact, the darkness was almost total, but they didn't dare turn on their flashlights and lanterns so as not to call attention to themselves. Pancho was quickly leading the way through serpentine tunnels as if he was very familiar with the path. That created a sense of security for the rest of the kids following quietly.

But the seven of them stifled exclamations, leaving their mouths gaping, when they turned a corner into beautiful and calming rays of light illuminating a small garden full of plants and flowers.

There was no one there. On the walls, there were colorful paintings illustrating scenes of ancient Aztec life: a marketplace full of people under the profuse light of the sun, a hospital where surgeons were conducting delicate cranial operations, observatories on high peaks where astronomers were examining the heavenly movements, great battles involving thousands of men on canoes and larger boats, cities with pyramids of varying sizes, gardens with quetzals, peacocks, other birds, serpents and jaguars.

The children, amazed, looked over the fascinating garden with reverence and great emotion. However, a nagging fear had enveloped them.

"Man, this looks great!" whispered Homero.

"Yes," Indra agreed, "this is the most beautiful thing I've seen in my life."

"It's great here," Erika said wistfully, finally relaxing.

"Look!" Thor suggested, pointing to the murals.

The murals were really animated, with people moving around, buying and selling. The volcanoes and mountain peaks shone under the resplendent sun, and the vendors' voices blended into the din of so many people and animals moving about. The commotion of the battle scenes produced dust clouds, with arrows, lances and projectiles crossing in the air. The two armies grappled with each other hand-to-hand, their drums beating wildly and their banners fluttering in the dust-filled air.

"Man, this is something else!" Thor exclaimed. "It's a thousand times better than our video games."

In the animated mural, the door to one of the pyramids was opening slowly. Behind it could be seen bright lights shimmering.

"Let's go," said Pancho.

"Where?" Alaín asked.

"That way," his friend answered, pointing to the door that was opening. "That's the rift between both worlds."

"The *what*?" Thor questioned, but Pancho was already leading the others to the murals.

The door to the great pyramid was completely open now, and the seven kids entered through it.

III

On the other side now, the kids were amazed once again. Before their very eyes was a patio of splendorous marvels. Giant stone blocks were covered in intricately designed, stylized serpents. There were also fountains surrounded by plants and flowers, tall sculpted statues covered in precious gems and lively colored curtains of fine cloths. There were tall *oyamel* and *ahuehuete* trees in which thousands of birds were chirping, including beautiful quetzals; they did not seem to fear the eagles perched at the top of the ivy covered mural. A pervasive calm filled the grand patio.

"My God, what is that?" whispered Indra, her mouth gaping.

"It's a dream," Erika stated.

"Yes, it's a dream," Alaín confirmed.

"No, children . . ." a voice echoed, ". . . this is the royal house of Señor Huitz."

The kids turned to where they heard the voice. Standing beside them was a tall, thin but strong man. He was almost completely nude except for short, red breeches and a hat made of feathers in the shape of a crown. He was more red-complected than brown and had a small beard. He had an earring in one ear, and his eyes, at that moment appearing like dim flames, looked at the kids through a hole in the *tlaqui,* or golden scepter, that he was carrying.

"Come with me," he told them, amused and smiling brightly.

The kids were petrified. Alaín was able to see out of the corner of his eye that Pancho seemed to be lost in a type of trance and that he was breathing heavily.

"But . . . who are you?" Erika asked defensively.

"I am Xiutecutli. Don't be afraid. Señora Tonatzin asked me to meet you as soon as you entered here."

Without thinking about it, Erika and Alaín turned to look at Pancho.

"Yes," Pancho said, his eyes half-closed and his breathing labored. "Let's go with him. He is the Lord of Fire."

"Don't dally," Xiute insisted. "There are some here who want to hurt you."

Hearing that, they all scurried to enter a large hall.

"Who wants to hurt us?" Alaín asked.

"And why?" Thor emphasized. "We haven't done anything."

"No one is supposed to come here," Xiute answered. "It's been sealed off for over five hundred years. When you entered, you disturbed many." Xiute paused, hearing the footsteps and movement of armed forces. "They're already here," he added, smiling enigmatically. "Get into my transport, but FAST."

"But what transport?" asked Homero.

"Oh, yes," Xiute said.

He made a circular gesture with his hand, throwing off sparks, and in that very moment, a type of carriage without wheels and made of pure flames appeared, suspended in the air.

"Wow!" Thor exclaimed.

"All right, get in," Xiute insisted.

"But it's burning up!" Yanira said.

"Nothing will happen to you," Xiute explained, warning that the footsteps were getting closer. "Children, what are you waiting for? Get in before it's too late."

They got into the carriage, amazed that the flames were not burning them, but instead felt soft and caressing. Xiute got in the front with his gold scepter and placed its orifice over a lever that he pushed. The carriage took off in the air slightly above the ground and flew through various empty halls. As they flew along, they heard continuous threatening sounds.

Thor was sitting next to Xiute, who was driving the vehicle with the same lever and asked, "How do you maneuver this thing?"

"With my *tlaqui*, of course," he responded, pointing to his scepter. "It's very easy. You just move it in the direction you want to go, to the left or right, or up and down, as you wish."

"How do you make it go faster?"

"You push the *tlaqui* down harder. If you want to go slower, you just have to rub it with your finger."

At that moment, they were going at a good clip. As they came out of a corridor, they passed a garden and entered another huge hall.

"Wow!" exclaimed Thor. "Listen, mister, could I please have a chance to drive a bit?"

"Maybe later," Xiute answered. "Right now, we have to be very careful. They're searching for us."

"Who is? How do you know?" Alaín interrupted.

"Can't you feel it?" Xiute asked them, really surprised.

"Yes, they *are* looking for us," Pancho said, still with his eyes half-closed.

"He sure can feel it," Xiute said as he turned the carriage into a corridor lined with giant stone statues, "but that's normal."

"Why is it normal?" Erika asked.

"Yes, why is it normal," Alaín repeated.

"Because Pancho is an Indian," Homero explained.

"I know how to drive," an insistent Thor interrupted them, "but my dad doesn't lend me his car. We have a Taurus and a Thunderbird. . . . But this machine here is a lot more efficient. Dad says I'm still too young."

"Who?" Xiute asked, smiling.

"My dad. But I'm thirteen years old, that's not too young."

"You're not too young, man," Homero commented, "you're fat."

"Keep out of this, you idiot."

"And why is this car made of fire, mister?" Erika asked.

"And why doesn't it burn us?" Alaín added.

"Well," Xiute answered as he pushed the lever down, which made the made the car's red flames more intense, "I am made of fire."

"Whoa!" Yanira uttered as the carriage was moving even faster now.

"They're here," Xiute suddenly announced.

"Who is?" Alaín asked. "I don't see anyone."

"There they are," Pancho said, his eyes almost completely closed.

Just then, they saw a group of men armed with heavy stone clubs who were blocking their path.

"Hold on," Xiute advised them.

The carriage sped up and crashed into the warriors, knocking them to the ground, and continued on its route.

"Strike!" Thor squealed. "That's what I call smashing!"

They were going super-fast now through large and seemingly unending halls of the royal abode.

"They're following us!" Homero yelled when he saw pursuing them five strange floating canoe-shaped vehicles carrying plumed warriors with shields.

"Who are they?" Alaín asked.

"They are *tlaloques*," Xiute answered, "who have a much lower rank than I do, but they can cause us problems. There's also some *mictlanes* from the underworld. Beware of them."

The warriors in the floating canoes were now shooting lances, arrows and some strange metal balls that were zipping by close to them.

"They's shooting at us!" cried Homero.

"With what?" Alaín asked.

"Let's get out of here!" Thor screamed.

"We'll shield ourselves," Xiute said, gesturing with his index finger, causing the projectiles to incinerate in the air as if passing through an invisible fire.

"Awesome, sir," Thor said. "How did you do that?"

"Oh, I just raised the shield."

"Oh, I get it," Thor said. "It's like in the movies, where spaceships have protective shields."

The projectiles continued to fall all around the carriage or burn up as they touched the shield, while Xiute continued to drive the speeding vehicle expertly.

"Oh, my God, why on earth did we ever enter these caves," Yanira uttered, pale from fear of the projectiles flying at them as well as from the speed of the car.

"It's horrible, isn't it?" added Yanira.

"Have you noticed how *handsome* this man is?"

"You should also hit the back, sir!" Thor commented. "Mister, where are your missiles? If you want, I can launch them."

"Be quiet, already, Héctor," Alaín challenged. "You sound like a braying burro."

"My name is Thor," Thor explained to Xiute. "And, you, you must think you're funny," he rebutted Alaín, who was laughing to himself.

"Well, it's about time we get rid of *tlaloquete*," Xiute said.

In an instant the flamed carriage came to a stop, but the floating canoes could not break fast enough and crashed into the invisible shield, quickly dissolving into thousands of sparks.

"Where did they go?" Thor asked upon seeing that the attacking canoes had disappeared.

"They evaporated," Xiute explained, smiling.

"Did you kill them?" Thor asked.

"No, they can't die. In a while they'll condense and recover their shape, but by that time, we'll already be with Tonatzin. Let's get going," he added. "There's no time to waste."

The kids noticed that Xiute had become very serious, as there appeared before them a very strong and robust man with long, straight hair that came down to his waist, shiny as if it was wet. By his side there was another being that terrified the kids. He was completely nude but covered in the blood-soaked skins of humans in varying degrees of decomposition. Both carried scepters.

"This isn't going to be easy," said Xiute.

"Who are they?" Alaín asked.

"The one with rain-splattered skin is Tláloc. His companion is Xipe Tótec. They've come for us, and it will be hard to escape them."

"What do they want with us?" Yanira asked.

"They want to take you to Huitz."

"Huitz? Who's Huitz?" Alaín asked. "You don't mean *Huitzilopochtli,* the god of human sacrifices, do you?"

"Are they gonna sacrifice us?" Erika interjected, terrified.

"That's what we're trying to avoid."

"Save us, mister, please," Yanira begged. "I think it's time to go home. I promise, we'll never come back to the cave. . . . I'll never even come back to Tepoztlán."

"They're going to try to break my shield," Xiute warned as the two beings slowly approached them. "If they break it, I'll try fighting them while you all escape. You can count on Tonatzin sending someone else to recue you and return you to the entrance."

The kids noticed that Tláloc was carrying small white balls, like compressed ice or snow. His eyes also appeared icy as, with great force, he threw one of the balls at them.

They felt a heavy blow reverberate from the shield. The kids started screaming in terror, feeling their vehicle shaking and emitting high-pitched squeaks. Xiute could barely maintain control of the vehicle, when another ball came at them at high speed. Xiute was able to shoot back a powerful stream of flames that dissolved the ball in midair, but because he could hardly control the carriage, he was not able to stop two more balls from hitting them.

"I'm getting all wet," Thor exclaimed as the vehicle's flames were quickly being extinguished and converted to bubbling water.

"Jump!" Xiute shouted. "I could stop the hit this time! Try to get away while I fight them."

The vehicle which had been reduced to hot water was bouncing up and down, and the kids jumped out, rolled on the ground, got on their feet and took off. Out of the corner of their eyes they could see Xiute using his scepter to fight Tláloc, who was wielding a solid ice sword, and Xipe Tótec, who was cracking a whip made of human hide. The three of them were beating each other savagely.

"Run! Run!" Pancho was shouting to his friends, who could not resist looking back at the battle unfolding behind them.

But it was too late. Xiute and Tláloc were locked in the fight, amid smoke, splashing water, flames and ear-splitting noise. Xipe Tótec was able to free himself and take a superhuman leap through the palace corridors and block the kids with his menacing whip that was dripping blood.

"We're done for!" Yanira was able to mutter.

"That's right, girl," Xipe sneered.

The sun was starting to set when Xipe Tótec stopped the kids, who now felt like all their energy had been drained. They were so depressed that they could not speak. Now and then, one of them would lift their downcast eyes to look at the others and almost feel the racing of their hearts in fear of what was to come.

Far off, Xiutecutli and Tláloc were still locked in battle, when a squad of warriors appeared, flanked the kids and led them to a large, open patio. They could see clouds gathering on the sunsetting horizon. Down in the town below, Indra was thinking, life was continuing as normal in what was sure to be a beautiful evening. How she regretted ever having entered that cavern that had placed them in danger of losing their lives.

Everything was so strange, Erika was thinking amid her fear. *How was all that happened possible?* Before she knew it, they had entered Tepozteco's belly, where they encountered the Aztec gods. Without a doubt these were the ancient divinities that everyone thought never existed. They were all very powerful gods, including the crazy old man who had transformed into a dog and peed on Thor . . . that one, at least, was amusing. . . . He had told them his name, but she could not recall it.

Erika could kick herself because she knew practically nothing about the Aztec gods. No one ever spoke of them, at least not in school. Why was that? After all, they lived in Mexico, and it was said that those were the gods worshipped by their forebears, their great-grandparents and great-great-grandparents, back to the most remote ancestors. And Tona, at first she appeared to them as a beautiful Indian, a kind mother, but of course, she had great powers . . . Tonatzin . . . Erika kind of remembered hearing about her sometime in the past . . . something about the Virgin of Guadalupe . . . *No way! It couldn't be!* It was better that Selene was still asleep . . . safe . . . or maybe not?

Yanira could not take her eyes off Xipe Tótec, who was marching in front of the guards, carrying his sharp, pointed scepter. His hair was combed back flat on his head with a part in the middle and two braids on the side. He was completely nude under his bloody, stinking clothing of human skin, which upset Yanira to no end. Poor Yanira felt abandoned and didn't have the will to escape or fight or anything. It also seemed like a dream to her . . . it just *had* to be a dream from which she would wake up soon, nestled in her own bed and not staring at those men in antique armor and with plumes on their heads.

They had now entered another wing of the palace, which was a small hall with mostly bare walls, except for two humongous dragon heads that were spitting flames from their mouths.

"You're going to stay here for a while," Xipe Tótec said with a mocking smile. "I'll come back for you later and take you to Huitz's hall."

"What are you all going to do with us, mister?" Erika inquired in a scared, high-pitched voice.

"Yeah, what are you gonna do with us?" Alaín asked weakly.

"You will all have the honor of being sacrificed to our Lord Huitz and his mother, her Highness Coatlicue. Get ready," Xipe Tótec responded, almost laughing and exited with his men.

The girls looked at each other and began to cry. The guys tried to be strong, but they also were obviously terrified.

"Alas," Thor whispered Alaín's nickname looking for comfort, "do you think they're serious?"

"We . . ."

"Well, we haven't done anything to them, have we?"

"I'm not sure . . . I would like to have done something," Homero said.

"What could we have done? They're too big . . ." Thor answered, about to cry.

"They're *gods*," a pale Alaín answered.

"But how could they be gods? Like, gods don't exist. . . . I mean, not in addition to God the Father."

"And the Virgin," Erika added.

"Let's pray," Yanira suggested.

"I don't understand any of this . . ." said Alaín.

"I would have liked to—I don't know—at least see well enough what was going on so I could recount it . . ." Homero insisted.

"Well, don't lose hope," Indra said, calming down a bit. "You'll be able to tell all about it, 'cause Tona is gonna help us."

"Je-e-e-e-eze, you think we're gonna get outta this, man?" Thor said hopefully. "No one is gonna believe what we've been through."

"And Tona is alone, and she's a *woman*," Alaín reasoned. "The one who had a better chance of saving us was that other guy, the one who called himself Xiute, but, you see what happened: he lost the fight."

"Xiutecutli didn't lose anything," Pancho interjected.

They all turned to look at him. He was acting very weird breathing through his mouth, his eyes half closed.

"I see it," Pancho added. "He engaged in a ferocious battle with my Lord Tláloc, nine times crossing their scepters without either one winning. The battle was so brutal that they caused tremors in the mountain."

"Yes, it's true," Thor uttered, "a little while ago I felt it shaking."

"It was the battle between fire and water," Pancho continued. "Tláloc wanted to extinguish Xiutecutli, and he for his part wanted to convert his opponent into steam. How magnificent they both were!"

They all gave Pancho puzzled looks.

"Finally," Pancho continued, "Xiute was cornering Tláloc with the flames shooting out of his scepter. That's when the skinned-covered Xipe Tótec returned with a group of his warriors and my Lord Xiute had to retreat, taking a giant leap upward and disappearing into thin air. At this very moment, he's with my mother Tonatzin, strategizing. Nothing has been lost."

"But how do you know all that?" Erika asked, somewhat desperate.

"Yeah, how do you know that?"

"I say this because I'm seeing it," Pancho answered with his eyes closed now.

"This guy is making me nervous," Thor said. "He's like a witch or something."

"*I am seeing it*," Pancho repeated, straightening up as if there was a presence standing in front of him. "Here they are!"

They all looked at each other, not understanding anything, until the hall filled with the fragrance of fresh flowers and they heard Tona's voice.

"Children, listen to me," the voice said, "they are going to come for you now and take you to Huitzilopochtli, and something will happen that must happen. But you should not be afraid: your salvation will take place by means you least imagined. The one we have all waited for is among you."

They all stayed very quiet, not daring to say a word, and then the voice was heard no longer. Alaín, ever perceptive, noticed that Pancho's eyes were now half-closed and he was sweating and breathing through his mouth. *What was that about?* he wondered to himself. His life-long friend was more and more surprising. Alaín realized that Coral's cleansing the night before seemed to have taken place an eternity ago. He also determined that, in spite of everything, Tona's voice had calmed them all.

They all remained quiet and one by one fell asleep, and when Alaín was also succumbing to slumber he was able to notice that Pancho had remained the same, with his eyes half-closed and breathing deeply.

They had not slept long, when the horrendous Xipe Tótec and his guards returned for them. The dying light of sundown continued to fade across the heavens.

The kids were taken to an enormous patio with a small pyramid in its center. From its ivy-covered walls and profuse vegetation, stone sculptures of eagles, ocelots and serpents peeked out. In the dimming light of sundown and the light of innumerable torches everywhere, the view was magnificent. A slight, cooling breeze accompanied the nightfall.

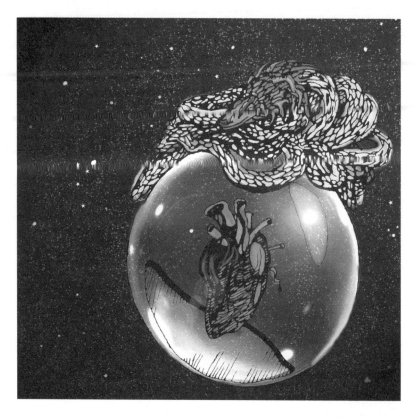

Up on top of the pyramid sat Huitz on a large throne. He was very tall, powerful-looking, dark-brown skinned and bedecked in splendor. Next to him stood Páinal, the deputy and messenger who always accompanied him.

There were many others crowded around. The kids were seated in front of the pyramid and they recognized Tona, barely keeping themselves from running and prostrating before her. Xiute, decked out in beautiful ornaments, stood next to her. They also recognized the fearful Coatlicue, and Chico or Chicomecóatl, and Chalch or Chalchiutlicue, and of course the powerful Tláloc Tlamacazqui and Xipe Tótec, who had climbed to the pyramid summit with the others. Among the ones the kids had not recognized were Coyolxauqui, old mother Temazcalteci, Lady Tzaputlatena and the beautiful Tlazultéutl with her sisters Teicu, Tlaco and Xucotzin. Next to them stood the gloomy Cihuapipiltis, who avidly inspected the kids because it was their custom to fly through the air and infect children with illness.

There, too, was Xochipilli, the Lord of Flowers; fat Omácatl who presided over banquets; dark Ixtlilton, Opuchtli the fisherman, Yiatecutli the merchant, Napatecutli the weaver and Lord of Pulque Tezcatzóncatl and his brothers Yiautécatl, Acolua, Tlilua, Pantécatl, Izquitécatl, Tultécatl, Papáztac, Tlaltecayohua, Umetuchtli, Tepuztécatl, Chimalpanécatl and Coluatzíncatl. There was also the Lord of Hell Mictlantecutli, his wife Micteca and their *mictlanes*, soldiers. Also present were the *tlaloques* and the remaining gods.

They were all attired in their most resplendent wardrobe, and Homero, despite the kids' lives being in danger, could not be more amazed at the sight.

With the backdrop of sundown, Páinal began to speak: "Tonight we have come together because something extraordinary has happened. After centuries of living in peace inside this holy hill, the seal that has isolated us from the world has been broken, possibly with assistance from some of us."

"Nothing of the sort," Xiute interrupted. "The seal was broken because it had to be. That is what was foretold."

The crowd began to murmur, but Páinal cut it off and said, "We'll get to that later. But it is evident that the prophecy has not come true, and you all know why."

"Ha!" exclaimed Chico, ironically.

By his side, Tona gestured for her to be quiet.

"In any case, today the path has been opened," said Páinal, "and these little humans found it. They found their way through an opening, helped undoubtedly by black magic, and we now fear that our peaceful retirement may have ended because of them."

"It's as clear as day," Xiute interrupted again, "that there was no magic in these kids finding the path . . . they're just harmless children."

"I am not a child!" Erika protested.

"But they are *yoris*," Tláloc responded.

"Not all of them," Chico clarified. "Can't you see?"

"What's a *yori*?" Thor asked.

"I think it's a *mestizo*," answered Alaín.

"In any case," Páinal continued, "none of that erases what is most important. The path has been opened and now anyone can find their way here to us. What should we do? That's the reason for this convocation."

"They must be sacrificed," Coatlicue affirmed emphatically, "no doubt about it."

Huitz, on his great throne, smiled, amused as he observed his mother.

"No, no!" Xiute cried out.

"Why not? It's our custom."

"No it's not, not anymore," Xiute insisted. "Our retirement was precisely because of this. And it's about time that we all realized that the sacrifices that humans used to make to us were good at that time, but things have changed so much that sacrifices don't make sense anymore. That's what our Lord Quetzalcóatl told us before he left, and that's what we transmitted through our dreams to the Toltecs of the world that still believed in us."

"But Quetzalcóatl fled," Huitz said, pointedly.

"He did not flee," Tonatzin responded. "He took a trip, which is not the same thing. He will return."

"He'll never return," said Coatlicue. "That enchanting coward fled from the incomparable power of my son."

"Ha!" exclaimed Chalch smiling enigmatically.

"Whatever . . . that's not the case in point," Páinal interrupted. "We have come together here to decide what to do with these little outsiders."

"Let's sacrifice them right now," insisted Coatlicue.

"No," replied Tona emphatically. "Let's take them to the opening so they can return to their world."

"No way!" Tláloc interrupted. "Are we going to let them go out and tell everyone what they have seen, and let our peace come to an end?"

"We could erase part of their minds so that they don't remember what they've seen," Xochipilli suggested. "I can donate my flowers of forgetting."

"Forget that! I want to feel their beating hearts in my hands!" Coatlicue demanded.

"Me too!" the spectral Coyolxauqui added. "It's been such a long time since I've had little hearts like theirs."

"Ah!" Huitz sighed nostalgically.

"It cannot happen," Xiute said. "Remember: we agreed that we were done with sacrifices. Don't forget the era of great darkness that came with the white, bearded men and their gods. Our faithful were decimated just for worshipping us. That was reason enough, but then we all agreed that a little worship in the form of a small, sincere and fervent offering was more valuable than the great shedding of blood, no matter how spectacular it was. That was no longer necessary."

"That was the right decision," Opuchtli said.

"How ridiculous!" Xipe shouted. "That retreat has made us weak and senile."

"That's right!" Mictlantecutli agreed. "It's time to return to our past glory!"

"Enough said. Let's sacrifice them and afterward we'll have a celebration," Omácatl proposed.

"I'll bring the drinks," Tezcanzóncatl offered.

"I'll bring the sleeping mats, like old times," Napatecutli said.

"Ah, the good old times!" Huitz sighed.

"In any case," Páinal interjected, "we can honor our commitments while being flexible in the face of unforeseen circumstance. . . ."

"What do you mean by that?" asked Xiute.

"We never thought that the whites, little ones or not, would invade our home. We should be flexible about sacrifices when it comes to the little humans."

"We need to do something with them, one way or another," said Tláloc. "Their presence here is causing conflicts that could be damaging to us. Just today, I had to fight Lord Xiutecutli. . . ."

"Who gave you a whipping," Thor said under his breath.

"Shhhh . . ."

"And it caused Tonatzin to disrespect me," Coatlicue added. "I would have never imagined such a thing!"

"It wasn't disrespect, Mother," Tona answered calmly.

"It was shameful! And don't dare think that you won't be punished for it, girl!"

"So, now we're going to argue like before," Páinal said, smirking.

"They need to be sacrificed, it's obvious!" Xipe Tótec shouted.

"No sacrificing!" replied Xochipilli.

"My brother Lord Huitzilopochtli should decide," Coyolxauqui proposed.

"Well, if you leave the decision to me . . ." Huitz started to say, when a powerful voice interrupted him.

"Just a minute, youngster, you can make all the decisions you want but not without hearing what I have to say about all this," Tezcatlipoca said.

He was no longer dressed as an old man nor a dog and was not drunk. He simply could not be seen; he was invisible. But his presence was so strong that everyone felt it and recognized it, including the kids who thought they saw a shadow in the direction of the voice.

"Oh, powerful god, who created heaven and earth, who gave life to men and call yourself Tezcatlipoca, Titlacahua, Moyocoyatzin, Yaotzin, Nécoc Yautl, Nezahualpilli!" exclaimed Huitzilopochtli, standing up. "No one intends to overlook you, especially not I, who is indebted to you for teaching me the arts of war and magic."

"Tezca? Isn't he the old man who we met in the cavern?" Thor asked Alaín softly.

"Yes. It's me, Chubs," Tezcatlipoca said. "And take care not to piss yourself again!"

Everyone, both gods and kids, broke into laughter as Thor blushed.

"Oh, father of us all," Páinal exclaimed, "state your piece. We will listen."

Tezcatlipoca remained invisible, but a shadow that kept growing denser was spreading over the pyramid.

"Listen to me," the powerful voice of the great god ordered. "It's easy to decide what we should do with these children. If they can be trusted, we should let them leave, and they could even be useful to us. If they are going to cause us problems, then we get rid of them."

All the gods looked at each other, weighing Tezcatlipoca's words.

"Very well, your lordship," Huitzilopochtli said, now very serious. "But how will we know if they are to be trusted?"

"Let's test them, of course," Chalch proposed. "It's the best way. I already did, and so did Chico. Listen to what I say: they're good . . . better than how they seem!" she added, amused.

"Let's test them," Tezca added. "It'll be entertaining, and we'll be able to find out a lot about the new world down below us."

All the gods remained quiet, deliberating the suggestion. The kids looked at each. Coatlicue, Huitz, Páinal and Tláloc were suspicious. Tona and Xiute looked serious but calm. Tezca observed them all with a knowing, bemused look.

Chalch was radiant. "That's an excellent idea!"

"Just a moment," a suspicious Huitz blurted out, "we have to think this over carefully. . . ."

"This is another of Tezcatlipoca's tricks," Coatlicue accused.

"Something smells rotten here," Tláloc confirmed.

"You're the one who smells bad," Chalch replied. "If you'd like, I'll give you some water so you can bathe."

"There's nothing wrong," Tezca said emphatically. "You can take my word for it."

"I don't think there is anything wrong with what our Lord Tezcatlipoca proposes," Tona interjected. "He's the oldest among us, the wisest . . ."

"And the biggest jokester," Coatlicue finished her sentence. "He's got something up his slee—"

"There's absolutely no trick," Tezca affirmed while smiling coyly.

"As far as I'm concerned, I see no problem in testing the outsiders. I listen and obey," Xochipilli said.

"Let's do what my father says," insisted Tzaputlatena.

"I agree," Opuchtli seconded.

"My sisters and I, too," beautiful Tlazultéutl agreed.

The rest of the gods also agreed, some of them unwillingly.

Only Coatlicue continued protesting. "He's playing with us, that old fox!" she warned.

"And you're a horrible old woman, shut your mouth!" Tezca spit out, still smiling slyly. "Well, now that we have all agreed, this is what we'll do: you all can observe the tests through my mirror."

"Just a minute," Tona interrupted. "There's one more little girl that I had set aside because she was so tiny. I'll bring her now . . . here she comes."

She made a gesture with one hand, blew softly on it twice, and a pastel-colored cloud began taking Selene's shape, asleep among her friends. Tona made another gesture, and the little girl woke up.

"Hey, what's up? Wow, I had a great nap," she said, looking around at her friends. "I dreamt that . . ." she paused, noticing the pyramid in front of them and the Aztec gods observing her. "Now what? Where are we? Where am I? Am I still dreaming?"

"Are you okay, Selene?" Erika asked.

"Yeah . . . Who are all those people?"

"Don't ask, you'll find out soon enough," Tona said.

"Ay! Here's that nice lady!" Selene exclaimed, content.

"I'll take charge of testing this little girl," Tona announced in a tone that left no room for discussion.

"I've already seen them all," Chalch said. "The most interesting one is that boy," she said, pointing to Pancho.

"I'll take charge of him," Tezca assented.

"I propose that the children each select whom they want to exam them," said Tona.

"And why is that?" Alaín forced himself to ask. "How are you going to test us?"

"What kind of test?" Erika wanted to know.

"Oh, you'll see, you'll see. You, go ahead and choose who you think will do it best."

"I choose that beautiful woman," Indra said, calmly pointing to Tlazultéutl.

"My name is Tlazultéutl, sweetie."

"Thank you."

"You, too, are very pretty."

"Enough of the cutsie stuff!" Tezca, commented. "Beauties are so vain!"

"I," added Homero, "choose Mister Xiute."

Xiute smiled, delighted, and nodded.

"And I," Yanira said, "choose Lady Chico."

Chicomecóatl likewise nodded.

"They're behaving so well," Chalch commented to Tona, who was by her side.

Tona agreed and, like the others, turned to the children.

Alaín looked over all the gods, then straightened up and said confidently, "I'm with Lord Tláloc."

"Very, very good!" Chalch said, while Tláloc was giving Alaín a penetrating look.

Erika was suddenly blushing.

"What's the matter?" Alaín asked.

"It's that . . ." Erika paused and then challenged, enraged, "I want Lady Coatlicue!"

"Waddya know!" Huitz laughed.

"Well, well, well . . ." Coatlicue commented, smiling enigmatically.

"That leaves only you, dummy," Homero said to Thor. "Who do you choose?"

"Me?" Thor responded, turning very pale, overcome with conflicting emotions.

"Yes, you. Wake up!"

"Well, I choose the top boss, who else but the great Huitzilopochtli!" exclaimed Thor, proud but at the same time trembling with fear.

"Oh, yes? You choose me? Well, now you'll see what for!" Huitz almost bellowed.

With that, everyone witnessed how in a matter of seconds Huitz had shrunk to the size of a dot and shot up and incrusted himself in Thor's forehead, just above his eyes. Thor's eyes

almost popped out of his skull. Something had invaded his body, soul and spirit, something so strong, so powerful, and he felt as if his entire being was expanding with such incredible speed that it couldn't be held within, and his body was about to explode.

"Get out of the way, boy, so I can see," Thor heard Huitz order from his insides.

"But, I'm not doing anything," Thor responded with his inner voice.

"Okay," Huitz's voice said, "don't move and especially don't think of anything. I want to see clearly throughout your body."

"That's so Huitzilopochtli. He knows no limits!" Tezca grumbled and had to raise his arm with stern authority.

Just at that moment, there were lightning flashes and thunder behind the pyramid, and then a giant circular mirror slowly emerged. Its surface was covered in smoke of various colors, which moved to the circumference allowing the looking glass to transform into a giant screen. On its surface could be seen what Huitzilopochtli was observing inside Thor and what Thor could see of the god. Huitz's view of Thor was like a dream: a volcano crater erupting and shooting out boulders, with torrents of bubbling lava flowing, fiery projectiles exploding into flames interminably. Crater stones were shot out amid giant flames and boiling lava flowing in high-pitched roars. The sky above was responding with thunder, lightning, wild downpours of rain and hail that barely dampened the terrible power of the volcano.

The kids observed Tezcatlipoca's smoking mirror, fascinated and terrified, full of sacred fervor, as the heavens waged war with the volcano. But they also observed their friend Thor, with his hair standing on edge, his eyes bulging but vacant and his rigid body covered in sweat. Huitz was nowhere to be seen because he was inside Thor.

On the screen then appeared an infinite collection of weapons: knives, daggers, swords, machetes, scimitars, lances, slingshots, clubs, chains, nets, armor, bayonets, pistols, rifles, shotguns, machine guns, bazookas, grenades, bombs, missiles, airplanes, ships, submarines, satellites, space ships . . .

On Thor's livid face appeared a slight smile, and from deep within someone spoke: "Hmmmmmmmm . . . how interesting . . ."

By then, the violent weather and volcano had converted the screen to a television showing a dizzying sequence of scenes: enormous airplanes raining down hundreds of bombs, missiles

being launched from mobile ramps, submarines firing torpe-
does that speedily cut through the waters, nuclear bombs that
became giant mushroom clouds on igniting, space ships firing
powerful lasers, planets exploding . . . Commandos clearing
their paths with bazookas, machine guns, pistols and knives;
juvenile gangs fighting each other with switchblade knives,
fierce children whose punches caused their schoolmates'
mouths and noses to bleed; police cars in high speed chases
shooting machine guns and throwing grenades; warriors decap-
itating their enemies with large swords or beating them with
axes and clubs; medieval armies who followed sieges by
breaking down castle walls with battering rams; swordsmen
winning their duels with their agile foils; giants and titans in
mortal combat; cartoon villains and monsters devouring children . . .

. . . And warrior gods: Mars, Thor . . . Huitzilopochtli!
There was Huitz. Thor perceived, *felt,* the terrifying Coatlicue
from within his mother's womb. Huitz observed the
Centzonhuitznahua men, who were angry that Coatlicue was
about to bear a child, and no one knew who the father was.
According to her, when she was sweeping one time, a feather
ball impregnated her. The Centzon Indians, led by
Coyolxauqui, didn't believe that one bit and decided to kill
Coatlicue and the child she was carrying: Huitz. Coyolxauqui
and the Centzons committed their crime, but Huitzilopochtli
sprouted from his mother's womb at that exact second, and the
first thing he did was go and slay his sister Coyolxauqui with
a torch made of serpents. After that, he defeated the Centzon
Indians and took away their weapons.

Thor and the rest of the kids watched as Huitz was becoming an exceptional warrior, the greatest, and Tezcatlipoca's
favorite. Tezca would take the young Huitz to Tula, making
him dance in the palm of his hand; afterward, they'd entertain

themselves as the unfortunate people threw themselves into a mountain chasm to be transformed into stones at the bottom. Old Tezca also taught the young god the greatest of magical arts, which in reality was no more than learning to manage his own natural powers. And Huitz became great at transforming himself into any animal.

In time, Huitz was accepted as the leader of the gods because of his incomparable ability as a warrior. Huitz would train his eyes on the heavens in seeking to dominate the most powerful forces, which were his own as well as those of the other gods and the entire universe. He was the eagle who had dominated the serpent. In the world below, the people rendered homage to him and honored him more than any other god. But his favorite people were the Aztecs. He accompanied them on their migrations from the North, showed them where to settle down in a true paradise and conquer the people who already resided there.

Thor learned everything about Huitz. He clearly saw the god through his spirit conquer the lavish city of Tenochtitlán, and on its main alter the chests of young men and innumerable prisoners were cleaved to offer their beating hearts to Huitzilopochli. Thor witnessed how Huitz transformed into a giant black eagle that inhaled the hearts offered up, from inside the eagle that was now both Huitz and Thor, and they both became blood-saturated air, very thick air. The eagle's eyes shone in the twilight behind the pyramid.

What a strange feeling to receive those hearts, Thor pondered; without a doubt the hearts provided energy, pure life; it was like getting drunk but maintaining control; it was like having a wild desire to show power, to conquer entire nations;

but it was also something indescribable; a pleasure beyond words that made him feel himself to be the entire universe, to feel all living beings existing within himself. . . . Of course! That's what being a god was, a very powerful god. And Thor also understood that so many who sacrificed themselves voluntarily were offering themselves to their god, in instants that lasted for *all* eternity, and when they died, they had the same sensation of all existent life in the universe, the unlimited energy of all the worlds and the very rare awareness that they too were gods during those moments.

Thor (and the other kids, thanks to Tezca's mirror) also observed that the sacrificed ones felt all of this because, since time immemorial, they customarily made cornbread shaped like Huitzilopochli and Quetzalcóatl. The latter "killed" Huitz, and the Aztecs therefore would break the bread of their god into pieces that they would eat because they were actually consuming the body and blood of their god. Huitz was not bothered by this; in reality, he approved that his children in the world would eat him and become part of him. What he did not like was that Quetzalcóatl was charged with killing him, even if it was only a religious ritual.

Thor realized then that Huitz and Quetzalcóatl were rivals and that they often had problems with each other, such strong conflicts that Quetzalcóatl decided to leave for Tullan Tlapallan, a place completely unknown. If he ever arrived there, no one knew.

Thor also realized that Huitz was unable to empower his people enough to expel the white invaders that one day had arrived with strange animals, firearms and incomprehensible gods. The Aztecs defended themselves with their characteristic valor, but the gods of the Spaniards were stronger and finally prevailed. However, it was not this alone. They were different from the Aztecs, who upon conquering a people respected the beliefs and customs of the conquered, and just required spoils and men to sacrifice. The Spaniards, on the other hand, destroyed every Aztec edifice, saying that the Aztec gods were barbaric demons and saw to it that the Indians lost everything, beginning with what gave meaning to their lives: their religion. And that's why the Mexican Indians closed themselves off, because for a long time they could not understand that all of a sudden, all at once, barbarically, all had changed for them. Only the new lady, Guadalupe, the good mother who so resembled the goddess Tonatzin, could comfort them and allow them to resign themselves to years of servitude and slavery.

Huitz and the other gods finally understood that they were having fewer and fewer believers in them and that is why they retreated to Tepozteco's belly. When they arrived there, they constructed another heavenly city. But they were sad, comprehending that they had lost all their faithful. They tried hard to adjust to the new reality in which a god that was three had replaced them. Their only hope was that one day, as it had been foretold, Quetzalcóatl, Huitz's great rival, would return from Tullan Tlapallan to Tepozteco. On that day, they would no longer be sealed in and they would be able to return to the world without being looked upon as devils nor useless antiques but true gods who could live alongside mother Guadalupe and the god that was three. They would all live together in Mexico.

With the exception of Tona and Chalen, the gods were sad, as were the kids, until they saw in the smoking mirror what Huitz now saw in Thor. He saw his house in Mexico City, his parents and all their problems, such strong arguments that they no longer spoke to each other, their paying hardly any attention to Thor, although they both loved him and he loved them even though at times he forgot about them as a result of his school and friends, his mischievous behavior and the large amounts of food and treats he would eat.

Everyone could see the innumerable little action figures he owned: space heroes and villains, fantastic wizards and demons. Thor also had a cuddle toy dinosaur on his bed; video games, mostly about war; music discs, an endless collection of movies and television shows. And they could also see reports of his soul, loaded with ghosts and little monsters but great energy and the ability to create things from scratch that were as yet undefined and useless. There was something luminescent and radiant in him that guided him through the large, dark labyrinth of being thirteen years old and still growing and changing rapidly.

Suddenly, the mirror was covered by light-blue smoke and from Thor's heart a tiny dot shot out that grew bigger and bigger in its trajectory and within a second turned into the majestic Huitzilopochtli sitting on his great throne. He was himself again, smiling with a mix of disdain and love.

"The little chubby one passes. He will never betray us, although at one time that might have been possible," Huitz attested.

Tona and Xiute smiled, satisfied.

And Thor was recovering from the experience. "Wow!" he exclaimed, "that was really cool. Like out of this world! Let me repeat, mister, that was c-o-o-ol! Let's do it again and again and again."

Everyone laughed.

Tezca commented: "He really is greedy!"

The kids looked at each other, puzzled, with a shy questioning smile. Somehow, they were no longer as afraid as before but instead pleased and even excited. Thor was radiant. And they eagerly subjected themselves to testing by the gods.

Tezcatlipoca's mirror allowed the gods and humans to witness the remaining trials. The terrifying Coatlicue penetrated Erika's body with the force of a hurricane, and she discovered a girl very strong in many things and weak in others, a girl who liked adventures, traveling around, debating and creating problems. Erika always wanted to be number one and was taken aback when she failed to achieve it. She was a whirlwind at home, and her mother tried to make her more feminine, but Erika was not attracted to boys nor makeup nor passing as older. Erika in reality *was* an old soul, capable of achieving *anything* she wanted, and that was that. In the mirror, everyone witnessed her stealing money from her mother's purse in order to play games at the arcade with the boys. And in sports, she was exceptional in volleyball, basketball and even baseball and soccer. And even at boxing! She'd put on the gloves and beat some of the boys her own age.

Erika was not aware of everything that was revealed about her during the test. She only became really embarrassed when it was shown that she really liked Alaín and Homero. But anyway, she was more terrified at having Coatlicue inside her. She was really uncomfortable feeling her inside her body. Coatlicue was enormous, showy and noisy. And Erika had no way of ignoring her no matter how hard she concentrated, no matter how she tried to numb those various parts of her body.

"Aha! Look what I've found here. This girl feels no shame!" Coatlicue commented, between guffaws that could be heard even outside the body.

Coatlicue only quieted down when she saw Erika would cry whenever there was something in her life she could not understand. Coatlicue also didn't like seeing the girl playing with dolls or snuggling up to her father because she adored him.

"What sentimentality," Coatlicue criticized.

Erika almost lost consciousness experiencing the awesome power of the goddess; she witnessed earthquakes, powerful hurricanes, volcanic eruptions—terrible, uncontrollable natural forces that were also full of life, movement and nurturing for all Earth's creatures. Coatlicue's fearsome features were only softened through her tremendous creativity. When Coatlicue finished her appraisal of Erika, all she said was that the girl was out-of-her-mind crazy, but a good person who could be trusted.

"I don't think I need a cleansing anymore," Erika said, very impressed.

The goddess of love Tlazultéutl entered Indra through her vagina, as would be expected, and everyone could see that Indra enjoyed extended baths, her mother's long massages, drying her hair for a lengthy period, applying makeup in secret, carefully selecting clothes made of expensive fabrics, chatting with her girlfriends, observing old women, and, of course, going out with boys. She was very pretty and, in addition, was so very attractive that young men of her age and even adult males noticed her. Some would explain to her that hers was a man's name, that of a Hindu god, and she'd seem even more enchanting. Tlazultéutl whispered in her ear that Indra loved men so much that she even had a masculine name.

Through Tlázul, Indra learned the great mysteries of love. She found out about things that she otherwise would have learned at a much older age. She learned that there existed a delicate pleasure that could even be experienced during menstruation, which she had already experienced and was much more different from what her friends and even her own mother had described. It had not been bothersome but instead fascinating. And she also found out that pleasure could be accompanied by pain, guilt and regret. It turned out that Tlazultéutl and her sisters were not only goddesses of love but

also the confessors of the Aztecs and levied severe punishments on the repentant.

Chicomecóatl manifested herself to Yanira as the goddess of sustenance, for she happily provided the food and everything else that was necessary. Chico, herself, was not interested in preparing the food nor cleaning house but instead administering it and seeing that all necessities were provided for and that everything was in its rightful place. She especially liked her crown, the vase and flower that never left her side.

Through Yanira, who was very bright but did not always show it, Chico learned a great deal: she realized that she, too, appreciated things being in order; that her strengths were organizing things, shopping and managing finances. Beyond that, Yanira had a pleasant personality, avoided envy and was not judgmental; she was approachable, wise, noble and very easygoing. Her greatest defect was that she was too interested in money. In the mirror-screen, everyone could see her secretly held treasures: foreign coins; her considerable, well-ordered savings accounts; a box with checkbooks, account statements and expired credit cards. One of her greatest desires was to have her own credit card, and her father had finally promised her one when she turned fifteen. How she hated waiting: another year and a half to go!

"She's clean as a whistle," Chico reported on abandoning Yanira's body. "She won't be a problem."

Tonatzin, followed, softly entering through Selene's mouth. The mirror clearly showed the little girl's soul, still populated with many small animals, cartoon and fairy tale characters, and a very vivid world of heroes, princesses, villains and dragons. The mirror-screen was full of dolls, Barbies and her parents. Her father appeared as a giant in his daughter's eyes, her mother as large as the house in which they lived. On the other hand, Selene was delighted to have Tona inside her; the goddess was infinite goodness, a perfectly pure and serene beauty, a natural mother with the perfect proportion of love and authority for raising children. She knew more than anyone else how to lull and console them, and she was happy cooking and cleaning house because she knew why they were necessary and what it meant to families; in addition, she had an infinite capacity for work. She was wise enough to know that each person had to follow their own path and that everything has its proper place in the world, especially religion. Tona did not spend much time with Selene.

"I'm finished examining this little girl even though there was no need. She is lovely," Tona explained.

Homero received Xiutecutli through his chest like something that split it open and inflamed it. His heart caught fire and he seemed to consume himself in flames, at once coming to understand the different levels of fire in the world: stars, immense igneous masses, their varied colors and beautiful shapes; from flashes in the pan to signal fires to protective warmth to illumination to fires that cook, heat, purify, burn, torture, destroy and consume everything, as well as those that blackout, barely glow and caress . . .

For Homero it represented
the world of art, poetry and
especially music, and that's why
Homero had created his own language and his own world, the
Third Universe of the Fourth
Cosmos, with all its stars, planetary
systems, satellites, worlds, peoples
and civilizations; all of this had him
somewhat confused, and at times
the histories and the historical figures, the great myths of the Third
Universe of the Fourth Cosmos
were all mixed up . . . Xiute's fire
was an invitation to soar to the
highest, it was a spiritual flame
aspiring to reach the heavens, that
needed to depend on something: if
there is no kindling, there is no
flame . . .
  . . . In Homero it was the desire
to live his thirteen years with a rare
intensity: rock music fascinated
him, the harder the better, and also
some classical music, for at home
there were many books and records.
He also was talented at drawing and
composed music for the poems he
wrote. He had an unbridled imagination, and that's why he'd spend so
much time alone; he also like being
with his friends, with whom he felt
safe, although still timid.

Tláloc penetrated Alaín's eyes, flowed from his tear ducts
into his veins and up into his brain, and then made his presence felt throughout the young man's mind and body.
"Boy, can you hear me?" Tláloc said from inside Alaín.
"Here I am. Stay calm, I won't hurt you."

"Yes, sir," answered Alaín, terrified.

He clearly felt Tláloc inside and understood that the god
could do whatever he pleased, starting by blocking his thoughts,
his ability to make decisions and govern his body. "How horrible it would be if I have an itch and this guy doesn't let me
scratch it!"

"Nothing is going to happen to you, once you stop those
stupid thoughts. You think too much. What you need to do
now is go with the flow."

Tláloc took over, and Alaín joined him in converting to
strong river rapids that would curve suddenly around large
boulders breaking the flow, turning it to foam. The current was
so strong that Alaín could barely resist the tremendous pressure
he had become. Then the river reached a waterfall that spilled
over from very high in what seemed an unending distance into
a grand circular lake at the bottom. It then flowed serenely
between broad banks along a picturesque landscape to the sea.
Alaín dove down to the ocean depths, where he saw an incredibly luminescent body of energy, the greatest live source of
power that was also linked to outer space, as this luminescent
power source was also accessible from the heavens and space.
Alaín understood that if he were successful in connecting to the
power source, he too would become a god, but he remained far,
very far from it, because the current that he and Tláloc were,
ascended very rapidly to the surface, became steam, condensed
into a cloud, began thundering, sending out lightning in powerful electric discharges and was undone in a loud, liberating
powerful storm pushed by strong winds and then returned to

the earth to bathe trees and fill wells and satisfy people's thirst, cook their food and nurture their crops.

❖❖❖

. . . While all this was happening, Pancho seemed unaware of everything. He still seemed to be sleeping and awake at the same time with his eyes half-open, his breathing heavy and irregular through his mouth. Alarmed, Alaín looked at him now and then, and it flashed into his mind that his friend was in a trance.

Pancho did not seem aware that he would be the last to be examined.

Tezca descended from the pyramid as a shadow and stood facing Pancho.

"Wake up, already!" he ordered in a strange voice. "You are going to find out who you are!"

"I know who I am," Pancho said as he opened his eyes wide.

"Who are you?"

"You know very well who I am," Pancho said, now with an assertiveness that astonished his friends.

"Do you remember everything?" Tezcatlipoca asked.

"Yes, it came to me all of a sudden when you spoke to me just now. But deep down I knew it when Chalch examined us. But, really, I've known it without knowing it since I was born."

"All right, tell us what happened. Where did you go, whom did you find, what did you see and hear, what are you going to do?"

Pancho immediately disintegrated and became a shaft of light that cut into the shadow that was Tezcatlipoca.

The smoke that covered the mirror withdrew to its frame and revealed a broad extensive city. It was the bustling city of Teotihuacán with its pyramids: some people constructing edifices, others crafting furniture and other objects, doctors tending to the ill, teachers educating and students learning, some writing poems or composing music or painting scenes from Aztec life in vibrant colors. There were warriors guarding them, merchants selling their wares, and in the temples priests and the faithful were attending religious services. Lines of young boys were waiting to be sacrificed on the altars. And suddenly, however, the heavens parted, and the sun seemed to descend upon the great city. It was Quetzalcóatl, the god who had been present at creation, the sun god, the lord of the winds, the king of civilization, Huitzilopochtli's great rival.

He reached down to the altars of sacrifice and ordered: "No more."

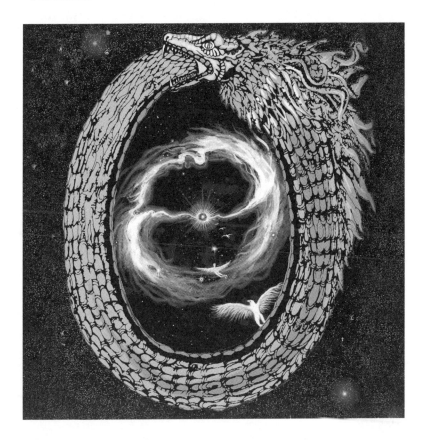

The priests did not know what to do. They invoked Huitzilopochtli, and he arrived, armed from head to foot. "Who dares interrupt the sacred services?" he roared. "This must end," Quetzalcóatl responded. "It is too bloody and cruel. And it no longer serves a purpose."

"You don't even exist anymore, nor do you live here. Now you're just a vision, an illusion," Huitz said, "Within a few centuries, you'll be searching for something you will never find. You are stupid and will never understand that my father Tezca and I tricked you."

"It may be that at this time it's just my image that's before you. But you're wrong: I will return, and when I do, everything will have changed."

Huitz mocked him, laughed at him, suddenly unsheathed his scepter and issued a powerful blow to his rival's image, which immediately withdrew to the heavens above.

"Don't run away! Always the coward!" shouted Huitz as he hurled lightning bolts at the image of Quetzalcóatl, which fended them off with his scepter.

"I'm no longer going to fight with you, Huitz," Quetzalcóatl said and became invisible again.

Huitz searched the entire sky for him but could not find him.

. . . After that, the young prince Ce Ácatl Topiltzin appeared as the child he was when his father had been assassinated and the usurper of the throne assumed power in Tepoztlán. In time, the prince reconquered the throne and avenged his father. Then, as King of the Toltecs he became Quetzalcóatl's priest, the god taking up residence within him; Topiltzin became Quetzalcóatl and left Tepoztlán to found Tula and bring abundance to his people. He subsequently became known as the rich and wise bearded king who disapproved of human sacrifice and spread wisdom as a solar being. One day, King Quetzalcóatl was tricked by Huitzilopochtli and Tezcatlipoca;

the king got drunk and was saddened to see himself as old. Tezca therefore advised him to go to Tullan Tlapallan, where an old one like himself was waiting to talk to him and that, upon returning, if and when he returned, Quetzalcóatl would be young again. Quetzalcóatl left, leaving behind signs of his body having passed by: new homes, temples, bridges and courts for ball games. He passed through the beautiful lagoons of Anáhuac and continued south until he encountered the Mayas, who called him Kukulkán. He taught them many things, he changed and enriched the spirit of the great people, but always told them that he was just passing through because the sun was calling him. And that is why he later crossed the sea, always searching for Tullan Tlapallan, a place unknown to everyone. He traveled over oceans and continents meeting the various peoples of the world and their gods, which surprised him greatly because he had always thought that he and his companions were the only gods that existed. But no: there were many gods, everywhere, and they all recognized Quetzalcóatl as a god and conversed with him or, like Huitz, fought him, forcing him to flee because he no longer wished to fight. He even thought of organizing a great meeting of all the gods of all the regions of the world so they could share their stories. But it proved impossible to do because he began to realize that he and the other gods in reality were all one, they were all the same one divinity who had adopted different forms and names in each period of time and region. That unitary divinity was like a flexible mold that could change shapes and names as many times as necessary to serve the needs of the faithful. He was beginning to understand that he was part of what existed everywhere, but that in one location, certainly Tullan Tlapallan, it was concentrated into an extraordinary, indescribable source of power.

❖❖❖

Quetzalcóatl continued his journey to the different points of the universe and met up with innumerable civilizations that were located far beyond our own world: the resuscitated of Riverworld, the engineers of Ringworld, the domesticators of the Arrakis desert, the asexual and hermaphrodite beings of Winter or Gueden, the planet of scientists of Asteroide Sargasso that transformed Gulliver Foyle into tiger-tiger. Quetzalcóatl observed the worlds of Trantor, Fantasia, Middle Earth, Narnia, Earthsea, Prydain, Worlorn, Melniboné and Borthan, including Sumara Borthan. He witnessed the dance of the stars and those same stars punishing the planets for attempting to change the stars' trajectories and use them as transports through space. He saw an infinite number of galaxies and civilizations with gods, only to conclude that he would never be able in the infinite expanse of the universe (which for some was quite close) to reach the strange luminous mechanism which was the source of power at its center as well as the circumference of everything that exists. He headed for that center but spent entire eons in attempting to reach it, at times passing through unimaginable future times, and at others beholding the origins, the very first grand explosion of life. He arrived, nevertheless, and despite the supreme power of the source, was able to go up to it and grasp the powerful light whose function was precisely to grab him. He then understood how limited his powers were as a god, how much he did not understand as a wise god. . . .

. . . He never learned how long he had been held by the power source, but he did realize that this fountain of power encompassed all of the universes and that through its spirit Quetzalcóatl could see everything, everywhere, at any time throughout time. That was when he easily found Tullan Tlapallan and concentrated on this old man who had waited

for him and who was none other than himself, the Quetzalcóatl who had always been there, whom he had missed since leaving Tula. The two of them fused into one and decided to return to Earth, to once again assume human form and enjoy it to the maximum, from the human ignorance of not even knowing who one is and the need to remember and confirm it. Just as it had been written.

The return route was very long, traversing innumerable time periods and places, but at the same time was very brief, hardly the blink of an eye, because Quetzalcóatl had to shrink to minimum size and transform himself into a sperm cell with a nucleus and place himself in his mother's womb, the orphan Guillermina who lived in Tepoztlán; Quetzalcóatl was once again human and was ready to be born. But he knew nothing about himself. He had forgotten everything. In Tepoztlán, no one knew who Pancho's father was, and his mother Guillermina could not explain how she had conceived a child. All she had were marvelous dreams of wonders she did not understand. She thought herself under a spell, and thus she explored herbs, witchcraft, healing, cleansings and divination in order to learn if she had been cast under a spell and by whom, and what she could do about it beyond caring dearly for her little son, whom she baptized as Francisco in honor of her own father.

Guillermina was continuously surprised by her son. He learned to walk at six months and to speak at seven; at two years old he would already take long hikes in the wilderness that would cause Guillermina fear to no end. That is how Pancho learned all there was to learn about plants by the time he was four, and his mother often asked him about things she did not know or remember. At the same time, Pancho appeared to be a perfectly normal boy. From a young age he sensed that he should not show his knowledge and abilities beyond those of a normal schoolboy, with the exception for his love of the Tepozteco, and that is how he knew more about it. That is how he became the first to discover how a landslide had uncovered the entryway to the city of the gods. And that is how he was able to discover his own destiny, which now was connected to those of Alaín and his city friends. He would never have imagined it would transpire that way but, of course, that is as it was meant to be.

Tezcatlipoca's mirror once again was covered by smoke and no longer showed anything. All the gods, including Huitz, were shocked beyond words. It was now evident to them that everything had changed and would no longer be the same. They would be able to leave Tepozteco and once again move about the great volcanoes and the old pyramids, and they no longer would bemoan their not having as many believers as before because, in their own way, they would live once again in the hearts of the Mexican people, beginning with those children who now knew them inside-out and who, to a large degree, were now part of them as well.

That is why it was no surprise that Tezca and Quetzalcóatl's shade transformed into a body of incandescent light and then dissolved into splendorous divine sparks until the gods appeared in all its splendor All the others, including Coatlicue and Huitzilopochtli, happily gathered around to greet and congratulate Quetzalcóatl, who had finally returned. He continued to appear as the teenage Pancho, but with such a difference!

IV

It was already nighttime when the seven city kids left the cavern. It had gotten late, and they had to hurry so as not to worry Alaín's parents. The kids had spent the whole day out! But they did not feel the least bit tired, and not even Selene and Thor were hungry. They all felt as if they had a new energy that permeated them from head to toe. With the aid of the lights they were carrying, they easily found their way down the trail, past the waterfall and along the narrow path around the mountain; they proceeded without difficulty even though Pancho was no longer there to guide them. He was not really needed because now they felt like they knew the mountain better than anyone.

Further down, they found Alaín's worried parents, who had organized a group of neighbors into a search party.

"Darn kids!" Alaín's father exclaimed on seeing them.

"You had us so worried! Did you get lost or what?" Coral asked as she hugged and kissed her son.

"We went into a gigantic cavern!" Selene said.

"It was incredibly large." Thor added.

"But we didn't get lost . . ." Alaín started to say.

"Nope, we didn't get lost," Erika took the words out of his mouth. "We always knew where we were."

"And Pancho? I don't see him."

"He stayed back with some friends he ran into up there," Alaín said with a straight face.

"That's right," Erika confirmed.

"What about his mother? Isn't she going to get worried?"

"Oh, she knows," Coral responded to the surprise of all the kids. "Before we went looking for them, I went by Guillermina's to see if she wanted to join us, and she said that the kids were coming back without Pancho . . . And that we should not worry because they were fine and on their way back. Can you believe it? How did she know?"

"Well, she's a witch, right?" Alaín's father laughed.

The seven kids were amazed.

"And what did you eat? Did you finish all the snacks?" Coral asked while hugging Alaín again.

"We had a feast," Thor answered, "stews, *mole*, blue corn tortillas . . ."

"Oh, sure, like going up to Tepozteco was like going to the marketplace," Coral said.

"No, really, we even had some snacks left over," Selene informed them.

"So, what did you see up there?" Alaín's father asked.

"We found . . ." Erika began to say.

"The Aztec gods!" Alaín was more than happy to finish her sentence.

"They're really neat," Yanira added.

"Divine," said Indra.

"Well, of course, they're divine, dummy," Alaín commented. "They're gods, right?"

"I'm going to write a long poem about all of that."

"What an imagination," Coral said.

"You see, I told you no one would believe us," Yanira uttered.

"There was no need for it," Homero affirmed.

"Somehow, these kids look changed to me," Alaín's father said.

"Yes," Coral agreed, "like, they're more lively."

"Señora, did a boy named Rubén call me from Mexico City?" Indra asked with a dreamy look and a *divine* shine to her face.

GLOSSARY OF GODS

Acolua (Acolhua)
One of the gods of *pulque** and drunkenness. These gods, together, were called *Centzon Totochtin* (four hundred rabbits). The name *Acolua* describes a person who has shoulders.

Ce Ácatl Topiltzin
Ruler and chief priest of Tula (Tollan). He took the name of the most important god as one of his titles: *Ce Ácatl Topiltzin Quetzalcóatl*.

Centzonhuitznahua (Centzon Huitznaua)
The four hundred children of the goddess *Coatlicue* (the supreme goddess of the earth), who represented the southern stars. They were brothers of *Coyolxauqui* (goddess of the moon) and *Huitzilopochtli* (god of war).

Chalchiutlicue (Chalch) (Chalchiuhtlicue; Chalchihuitlicue)
Goddess of rivers, lakes, streams and other fresh waters. Wife (in some myths, the sister) of the rain god *Tlaloc*. He was associated with snakes.

Chicomecóatl (Chico)
Goddess of sustenance and corn. She is often depicted in sculptures holding a double ear of corn in each hand.

Chimalpanécatl
One of the gods of *pulque*. These gods, together, were called *Centzon Totochtin* (four hundred rabbits). The name *Chimalpanécatl* describes a person from Chimalpán.

---

* *Pulque*, or *octli*, is an alcoholic beverage made from the fermented sap of agave. It is a traditional beverage in central Mexico, where it has been produced for thousands of years. It has the color of milk, a rather viscous consistency and a sour yeast-like taste.

Cihuapipiltis (Cihuapipiltin)
The spirits of women of the ruling class who died during their first childbirth. These spirits returned to the world of the living on specific days of the year and caused evil, disease and sometimes death.

Ciguas (Sihuanaba; La Sihuehet; o Siguanaba, Cigua o Cegua)
The *Cigua* is a spirit that changes its physical appearance to deceive men. Seen from behind, she appears to be an attractive woman with long hair. When she turns around, her face is that of a horse or a skull.

Coatlicue
Supreme goddess of the earth. Creator and destroyer, mother of gods and mortals, patroness of childbirth and associated with war, government and agriculture. Mother of *Huitzilopochtli* (god of war), *Coyolxauqui* (goddess of the moon) and the *Centzonhuitznahua* (who represented the stars of the south).

Coluatzíncatl (Colhuantzíncatl)
One of the gods of *pulque*. These gods, together, were called *Centzon Totochtin* (four hundred rabbits). The name *Coluatzíncatl* describes a person from Colhuacan.

Coyolxauqui (Coyolxauhqui)
Goddess of the moon or the Milky Way. Daughter of *Coatlicue* (supreme goddess of the earth). Sister of *Huitzilopochtli* (god of war) and the *Centzonhuitznahua* (who represented the stars of the south).

Huitzilopochtli (Huitz)
God of the sun and war, considered the patron diety of Tenochtitlán. Associated with gold, warriors and rulers. Son of *Coatlicue* (supreme goddess of the earth). Brother of *Coyolxauqui* (goddess of the moon) and the *Centzonhuitznahua* (who represented the stars of the south).

Ixtlilton
God of health and medicine, specifically with regard to children. Brother of *Xochipilli*. He was also a god of dance and a soothsaying deity.

Izquitécatl
One of the gods of *pulque*. These gods, together, were called *Centzon Totochtin* (four hundred rabbits). The name *Izquitécatl* describes a person from Izquitlán.

Micteca
The assistants of the god *Mictlantecutli* (ruler of Mictlán: the underworld), who were tasked with digging a well so that *Quetzalcóatl* (the creator of the world and humanity) would fall into it when he tried to leave Mictlán.

Mictlanes
The nine levels of Mictlán (the underworld) which soul descend, in a journey lasting four years, until finally reaching extinction at the bottom.

Mictlantecutli (Mictlantecuhtli)
God of death. Ruler of Mictlán (the underworld). He was worshipped and feared throughout Mesoamerica and was closely associated with owls, spiders, bats and the cardinal direction south.

Napatecutli (Nauhpa; Tecuhtli; Nappatecuhtli; Nappateuctli)
One of the gods of Tlaloque. It was believed that he was the one who made reeds grow with the rain, for which he was also considered the patron deity of cane mat weavers.

Omácatl
This was the calendar name for *Tezcatlipoca* (the supreme god of the Aztec pantheon), an omnipotent and often malevolent deity associated with feasts and revelry. Omácatl was sometimes depicted as a large bone made of amaranth dough that people ate during festivals in his honor.

Opuchtli (Opochtli)

One of the gods of Tlaloque. He was the patron deity of those specializing in fishing and other sustenance-related activities in water. He was believed to have invented the fishing net, the three-pronged fishing harpoon, the stick for propelling canoes, the trap for catching waterfowl and other tools for the art of fishing and water hunting

Páinal (Paynal)

Messenger of *Huitzilopochtli*: a runner

Pantécatl (Patecatl; Pahtécatl; Patécatl)

God of medicine, healing, fertility, *pulque* and the discoverer of peyote. Father of the four hundred gods of pulque (the *Centzon Totochtin*, or four hundred rabbits).

Papáztac

One of the gods of *pulque*, specifically the god of its foam. These gods, together, were called *Centzon Totochtin* (four hundred rabbits). The name *Papáztac* describes a person drained of energy or vitality.

Quetzalcóatl (Kukulkán)

Feathered serpent god identified as Quetzalcóatl by the Toltecs and Aztecs and as Kukulkán by the Yucatecan Mayans. Creator god and life god. He was believed to have implemented many cultural innovations and then to have left peacefully, promising to return one day.

Teicu

One of the sisters of the four-part goddess *Tlazultéutl Ixcuina* (deity of sexuality, among other things). These four sisters were goddesses related to different aspects of sexuality.

Temazcalteci (Tema)

Goddess of steam baths (*temazcal*). She is often depicted with black rubber paint around her mouth, sometimes also covering her nose. This image could personify the steam bath itself, with her mouth representing its entry and exit points.

Tepuztécatl (Tepoztécatl)
One of the gods of *pulque*, specifically the god of fermentation. These gods, together, were called *Centzon Totochtin* (four hundred rabbits). The name *Tepuztécatl* describes a person from Tepoztlán.

Tezcatzóncatl (Tezca, Titla)
One of the gods of *pulque*. These gods, together, were called *Centzon Totochtin* (four hundred rabbits). The glyph (or symbol) representing the name *Tezcatzóncatl* seems to allude to the countless bubbles that form on the surface of fermented *pulque*.

Tlaco
One of the sisters of the four-part goddess *Tlazultéutl Ixcuina* (deity of sexuality, among other things). These four sisters were goddesses related to different aspects of sexuality.

Tláloc Tlamacazqui
Tláloc was the husband of Chalchiutlicue and the god associated with water-related weather conditions (rain, clouds, storms, floods, lightning, snow, ice and even droughts). *Tlamacazqui* means priest or servant of the temple.

Tlaloque
The gods of *Tlaloque* were a group of mountain gods associated with water, who were ruled by *Tláloc*. The *Tlaloque* were seen as parts of *Tláloc* and deities in their own right.

Tlaltecayohua
One of the gods of *pulque*. These gods, together, were called *Centzon Totochtin* (four hundred rabbits). The name *Tlaltecayohua* refers to falling earth.

Tlazultéutl (Tlazolteotl)
Goddess of sexuality, vice, lust, uncleanliness, purification, fertility, childbirth, divination and health. She was called *Tlaelcuani* (eater of filth), in charge of consuming the muck of the world and seeding the earth, and also played the role of cleanser of human impurities.

Another name of hers was *Ixcuina* (defender and protector of publicly shamed individuals and adulterers).

Tlilua (Tlilhua)
One of the gods of *pulque*. These gods, together, were called *Centzon Totochtin* (four hundred rabbits). The name *Tlilua* describes one that has black ink.

Tonatzin (Tona; Tonantzin)
Earth goddess symbolically connected to fertility and earth. Her name means "Our Mother." She embodies the loving, Mother Earth archetype, who gives us everything we need and who supports our every steps.

Tullán Tlapallan (Tollan)
Tullán was the original name of Tula, the city of Ce Ácatl Topiltzin. "Tlapallan" itself alludes to color. It is often found next to place names. Together, these "Places of Color" as they are known could be any place where cycles occur. *Tlapallan* and *Tlillan Tlapallan* were also used interchangeably to describe the place where *Topiltzin Quetzalcóatl* would go to die.

Tultécatl (Toltécatl)
One of the gods of *pulque*. These gods, together, were called *Centzon Totochtin* (four hundred rabbits). The name *Tultécatl* describes a person from Toltitlán.

Tzaputlatena (Tzapotlatena)
Goddess of Tzapotlán. She was believed to have discovered *uxitl*, or *oxitl*, a medicinal resin, and was thus the patron diety of collectors of this resin.

Umetuchtli (Ometochtli)
One of the gods of *pulque*. These gods, together, were called *Centzon Totochtin* (four hundred rabbits). The name "Umetuchtli" itself is often associated with an image of two rabbits in mexica mythology, so some sources consider him the leader of the *Centzon Totochtin*.

Xipe Tótec (Xipe)
God of spring, seeds and sowing, and the patron of metal workers (especially goldsmiths) and gemstone workers. Brother of *Tezcatlipoca*, *Huizilopochtli* and *Quetzalcóatl*. He was also associated with death, and thus was sometimes considered to cause disease.

Xiutecutli (Xiute) (Xiutecuhtli)
God of fire associated with young warriors and rulers. It was believe that, wherever there was fire, there was *Xiutecutli*.

Xochipilli
God of summer, flowers, pleasure, love, dance, painting, feasting, creativity and souls. He was also associated with butterflies and poetry. Brother of *Ixtlilton*.

Yiatecutli
He was the patron deity of merchants who traveled through the province of Anáhuac looking to trade goods.

Yiautécatl (Yautécatl)
One of the gods of *pulque*. These gods, together, were called *Centzon Totochtin* (four hundred rabbits). The name *Yiautécatl* describes a person from Yauhtlán.

Xucotzin
One of the sisters of the four-part goddess *Tlazultéutl Ixcuina* (deity of sexuality, among other things). These four sisters were goddesses related to different aspects of sexuality.